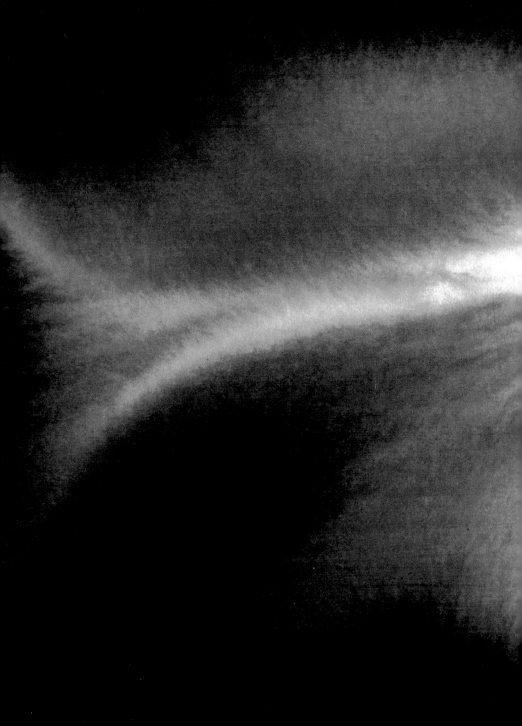

Dark Times

Rob Reger *and* Jessica Gruner

Emily®
the Strange

Dark Times

Illustrated by
Rob Reger

HARPER

An Imprint of HarperCollinsPublishers

Emily the Strange: Dark Times

Copyright © 2011 Cosmic Debris Etc., Inc.

Library of Congress Cataloging-in-Publication Data

Reger, Rob.

Dark times / Rob Reger and Jessica Gruner ; illustrated by Rob Reger.
— 1st ed.

p.   cm. — (Emily the Strange)

Summary: Traveling in her homemade Time-Out Machine, Emily
journeys to the eighteenth century to uncover the truth behind a Strange
family rumor.

ISBN 978-0-06-145235-2

[1. Time travel—Fiction. 2. Great-aunts—Fiction. 3. Family—
Fiction. 4. Supernatural—Fiction. 5. Adventure and adventurers—
Fiction. 6. Goth culture (Subculture)—Fiction.] I. Gruner, Jessica.
II. Title.

PZ7.R2587Dar   2010   2009032256

[Fic]—dc22   CIP

                                                                AC

Typography by Amy Ryan

11   12   13   LPR   10   9   8   7   6   5   4

❖

First Edition

dedicated to Wilder Waters

Sept. 1
Duntzton: Another town, another diary . . .

Have been busy busy busy with packing, moving, and unpacking my stuff, but FINALLY made it out of the house this evening to scope our new town and pick up some back-to-school supplies[1]— just the basics:

1. New journal (1) (obviously)
2. Assorted pens & pencils (red & black ONLY)
3. Glue (1 gal.)
4. Structural assay parsers (10)

---

1 Not that I have any intention of using these supplies at an actual SCHOOL.

Self-portrait with school supplies!

5. Watercolor paints (13 sets)
6. Folders (3)
7. Assorted test tubes (3 doz.)
8. Bunsen burner (1)
9. Sticky notes (baker's doz.)
10. Rolls of tape (1 gross)
11. Biomass (66 lbs.)
12. Index cards (3 doz.)
13. Driveshaft (1)

Some of these items are direly needed for construction of a new PrimevilPowerCase®. Having only one PPC® has become a huge bummer lately since I can only use it to power one major invention at a time. That's all well and good until I decide I want my Oddisee™, my Ambiplasmatron©, and my Tilt-A-Girl™ functioning simultaneously.[2] And unfortunately some of these parts are super spendy, not to mention hard to find in the sort of backwater towns Mom and I usually find ourselves in.[3]

Anyway, have decided it is high time I put together at least one more PPC®. Have introduced myself to Mr. Wilson, owner of

---

2 If only I hadn't used up all the liquid black rock I brought back from my ancestral home! That stuff was genius for powering whatever kind of crazy machine I poured it into.

3 Dumchester, Ridicaville, Tootleston, Blandindulle, Silifordville, Duntzton . . . I think the names say it all.

the local hardware store, which also happens to be the local thrift store, the local sundries store, and the local antique store. Man, Duntzton is small. Made arrangements for after-hours shopping, access to special-order catalogs, AND a student discount.

Regrettably, Wilson insists that I show some current student ID to receive said student discount. Even more regrettably, I have no student ID more recent than sixth grade. I did try my usual M.O. of introducing the owner of the local hardware store to my golem. Typically, this results in the owner falling hopelessly under the spell of Raven's bewitching beauty and giving me the biggest possible discount on purchases, with no ID needed. Wilson appears immune, however. Maybe he already likes someone else, or maybe the parched husk of his shriveled

ESPrints

3

Wilson and Raven.
No love connection here!

soul understands nothing of LURRRRVE. Blagfarx!

Am now considering getting enrolled in school, if only for the ID. Chances are pretty slim that the Duntzton educational system has much else to offer me. Nothing against Duntzton, you know. It's school as a general concept that doesn't agree with me so well. Though I should be perfectly honest and say that due to the success of my lifelong efforts at avoiding school, I have only spent 13 days in actual classes. (Summary below.)

1. Kindergarten, Day 1: Horrible shock to my system as I realized that unless I did something to avoid it, my year would be spent learning to stand in line, raise my hand before speaking, and share the safety scissors.
2. Kindergarten, Day 2: Was expelled from school for vandalism. Hey, I was young.
3. First Grade, Day 1: Left school with severe (severely FAKE!) case of scurvy.[4]
4. Fourth Grade, Day 1: Was excused from school due to lice.[5]
5. Fifth Grade, Day 1: Determined to make a real go of school this time.

---

4 I'll always have a fond place in my heart for that scurvy, which baffled doctors in three towns by resisting even the most determined doses of lime juice and vitamin C tablets, and kept me happily out of school through the third grade.

5 Actually very small robots I programmed to stay in my hair until mid-June the following year.

6. Fifth Grade, Day 2: Was expelled from school for vandalism. Hey, I was still young.
7. Sixth Grade, Day 1: Dragged myself to classes yet again.
8. Sixth Grade, Day 2: Continued to endure general school-related torment as stoically as possible.
9. Sixth Grade, Day 3: Was excused from classes when a tornado destroyed most of the town. Sometimes you just get lucky.
10. Seventh Grade, Day 1: Started school with open-minded attitude (and excellent Plan B).
11. Seventh Grade, Day 2: With heroic generosity of spirit, gave school another chance.
12. Seventh Grade, Day 3: Was expelled from school for possession of a contraband item.[6]
13. Eighth Grade, Day 1: Was sent home owing approx. 1 million hours in detention for various "crimes" (mostly sass-related). Later, town officials decided[7] that I did not need to attend classes.

It's not that I object to education. Not at all. I just haven't found any in the schools I've been to so far. But I do want that ID, and

---

6 My trusty slingshot. Clearly, they were looking for any opportunity to see me gone.

7 "Decided" = "were bribed to agree."

I don't mind at least checking out the Duntzton school. You never know—maybe they've got a wicked science lab, experimental music program, or slingshot range. And lots of Nobel Prize–winning teachers on staff. And night classes. And no other students. Yeah.

Anyway, I'm going to wait for daylight and pay them a visit. Mom has been absentmindedly mentioning school for the past three days, so I may as well get a jump on the whole business and lay the groundwork for getting myself enrolled and (if the school doesn't completely thrill me) subsequently excused for the year. No point in ruining a perfectly good autumn, winter, and spring with a lot of early wake-up calls, meaningless desk-warming, and insufferable people my age.

Later

Have unpacked and decorated my room, with expert help from Raven. Am patting self on back for perfecting her programming to this point. She is so well tuned these days that any outsider would think I was psychically commanding her. I might even say that she's showing some initiative of her own. For example, when Sabbath was making a toilet out of my packing materials, and Miles was leaping from crash-test dummy to antique birdcage to taxidermied rhino in unfettered glee, and Mystery was yakking up some liquefied strapping tape, and Neechee was generally making a feline happytime carnival out of the unpacking and decorating effort, Raven went right downstairs to the kitchen and yelled **"LIVER!"** in that huge booming voice she has sometimes. Which got all four cats out of the room about five seconds before my head would have exploded. Now THAT'S earning her keep!

Later

OK, it's finally business hours, am off to enroll myself in school.

Later

Visit to Duntzton school has been somewhat discouraging. Am glad I had my spy camera with me so I could document the

terrifying spectacle that greeted

me: — — — — —→

Her name was Carol. Carol does not work and play well with others.[8]

ME: Hi, Carol. I'm here to enroll myself in school.

CAROL: Your parent or guardian has to do that.

ME: I'm emanci-pated, so I am my own guardian. And I'm here to enroll myself in school.

CAROL: Let's see your documentation.

ME: [Handing over my papers.[9]]

C: This says you were emancipated when you were three years old.

---

8 Normally I'd appreciate this, as long as the person in question works and plays well with ME.

9 Totally authentic, by the way.

ME: Yep.

C: Get out of my office, you!

No worries. I did not really need to enroll in school to get an ID. Am moving on to Plan B.

Later

Success! I am now the proud bearer of a Duntzton school ID. Here's how that went down:

1. Left Carol's office and wandered halls for a while.
2. Liberated a lonely-looking clipboard from an unsupervised supply closet.
3. Stationed self outside random classroom, ear to the door.
4. Listened until teacher hollered a student's full name in that voice no school-age person can mistake for anything but the abject desire to be rid of Said Student.
5. Entered said classroom, consulted clipboard, and summoned Said Student to the principal's office.

alternative photo advance twist

LENS

download/printer cable

My lovely spy-cam!

ballpoint technology

photo advance button

6. Waited for Said Student to be excused and to gather possessions.
7. Closed the door behind us, then requested Said Student's ID.
8. Patiently listened to Said Student's vulgar protests and threats of violence.
9. Gently explained to Said Student some of the more thought-provoking consequences of my request not being immediately granted.
10. Collected student ID.
11. Wrote Said Student a rock-solid pass excusing attendance at school for the rest of the day.
12. Promised to return ID soon.
13. Took ID home, and within five minutes had crafted this lovely gem:

Later
You know how they say life imitates art? Well, in my case, life also

imitates lies.[10] For example, it's always been my habit, whenever some Adult inquires why I'm not in school, to casually respond, "Oh, I'm homeschooling myself." I swear, if you say something casually enough, I don't care how nonsensical it is, no one will question you. Anyway, I think that this year, I'm actually going to homeschool myself. If I present it to Mom as a done deal, she's not going to complain. Hey, it's better than me getting expelled again.

All right. Have had enough daylight today to last me for ~~months years~~ the rest of my life. Am going to bed.

Sept. 2

Today's assignments:
- Place orders for PPC® components—13 points
- Fingerpaint portrait of Black Cat Posse—13 points
- Make copy of Mom's house key—13 points
- Practice grapples and groin kicks—23 points

Have been to see Wilson at the hardware/antique/thrift/sundries store and put in my special orders. He was fairly abrasive, but it was a different kind of abrasive than the QUITE UNLIKABLE Carol down at the school, who is clearly mean to people because it brings joy to her petty little soul. No, Wilson is the kind of

---

10 Of course, the way I lie, it's an art.

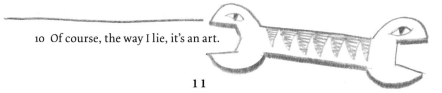

Grouch who simply has a Low Opinion of people in general, and therefore can't be bothered to Make Nice. And who am I to argue with that?

He delivered many scathing remarks about the oddness of my special orders. Remarks that only got more and more scathing the harder I laughed. In the end, having failed to put me in a bad mood, he demanded my student ID, then told me he was going to hold it until my orders arrived. What the flambams, I only made that thing for him anyway. I hope he enjoys looking at it for the next six to eight weeks!

Later

Found out at dinner that Mom called the school today and learned that I did not actually succeed in enrolling myself in classes. I had to explain what happened with Carol.

MOM: She said WHAT? That's ridiculous! I'll go down there myself tomorrow.

ME: Whoa there, Patti, I've got a better idea. You keep promising me we can try homeschooling. How about now?

M: Oh, sure, it's just so much paperwork, and . . .

ME: Actually, I turned in all the paperwork earlier today.

M: Oh. I see.

ME: And I wrote up a really great curriculum for the year. Here we go: Current Developments in Particle Physics, Advanced Practicum in Krav Maga, Complex Number Theory, Great Poetry of the Thirteenth Century, and Fingerpainting.

M: Don't you mean Figure Painting?

ME: Nope. Fingerpainting.

M: You can take <u>Fingerpainting</u> for school credit?

ME: You can take Fingerpainting for COLLEGE credit.

M: But who's teaching you these classes? I mean . . . I'll fingerpaint with you, and discuss poetry, but when you get going on particle physics, I start to bleed from the ears.

ME: I'll be going to this place downtown for the Krav Maga. What's it called . . .

NeeChee

Sabbath

Mystery

Miles

oh, Fight Club, very clever. Complex Number Theory—private lessons from a retired professor who lives two blocks from here. Great Poetry—online. Fingerpainting—uh, self-taught. And Particle Physics is mostly out of books and scientific publications. Now, if Duntzton HAD a particle physicist, I'd go talk to her. But they don't.

M: Well . . . but . . . I always kind of thought that if we ever actually tried homeschooling, I'd get to teach you a class myself.

ME: Sure thing, Patti. What are you an expert on?

M: Music theory, to begin with. You may shred on the guitar, but you still have a lot to learn.

ME: Fine. Are we good, then?

M: I think you could handle another academic subject. Maybe history?

ME: Could you narrow that down? This is a three-credit class, and history's kind of . . . big.

M: K. Let me think about it and I'll get back to you.

My new music theory teacher!!

Later

Am not sure whether to feel grumpy or excited about Mom teaching me history. I guess it's all going to depend on her approach. I mean, I don't mind a little history—certain parts have been fairly wicked. I even went to the trouble of building a Time-Out Machine a while back so I could go experience for myself some glories of the past. You know: Manhattan, 1974—the Ramones' first show. Flamjax, that was awesome. Dawning of the Mesozoic era—I do love me some archosaurian reptiles. And Mom's 13th birthday party—just in case I ever need blackmail material.

ESPrints

The Glorious T.O.M.!!!

Anyway, so what I'm saying is, I hope Patti is planning something AT LEAST equally exciting for this history class.

Later

Have been avoiding completing my assignments. Assignments that I assigned myself. SIGH. Am truly a procrastinator to the bone. TO THE BONE!!! Here's what I have been doing instead:

1. Rasslin' with kittycats.
2. Reorganizing record collection.
3. Programming Raven to reorganize my record collection.
4. Programming Raven to take care of various cat messes for me.
5. Lying on bed, staring at ceiling.
6. Installing secret compartments in walls and under floorboards of my room.
7. Filling secret compartments with secret items.
8. Writing menu of foods to be served at Yreka Bakery (e.g., strata tarts, snub buns, and naan).
9. Writing list of hairstyles to be offered at Nola's Salon (e.g., the Racecar, the Madam, and the Bob).
10. NOT writing list of products to be sold at Elite Tile.
11. Reengineering fuel duct shroud on Ambiplasmatron©.
12. Using Complex Number Theory textbook to exercise my triceps.
13. Halfheartedly testing various concoctions (tar, crude oil, extremely strong espresso) as substitutes for liquid black rock. No dice. Am hardly surprised.

Later—daybreak, time for bed

Mom has just been in to announce that she will be teaching History of the Strange Family. First class will be tonight. Am not exactly ecstatic with this choice of topic. I mean, I know some cool stuff about my Great-Aunt Emma, and I like Great-Aunt Millie just fine, but I fear that I am in for some excruciatingly tiresome lessons on long-dead relatives with whom I have nothing in common. GAHHH. Am going to sleep.

Sept. 3

Today's assignments:
- Return Said Student's ID—3 points
- Teach Sabbath location of litter box—13 points
- Make copy of Mom's house key (LATE!!)—13 points
- Practice grapples and groin kicks (LATE!!)—23 points
- Endure first session of Strange Family 101—63 points

Woke up at nightfall and ate dinner with Mom. Somewhat grumpy at prospect of history class tonight. Am working on plans to get myself excused from it for the year. If only I had the components for the spare PPC®, I could get the Time-Out Machine working without disabling my Oddisee. Then I could simply inform Mom that I am meeting my history requirements with good old-fashioned time travel. Oh flabberfarks!!! I keep forgetting[11] that the T.O.M. requires liquid black rock to operate. Liquid black rock that I do not have. Grrr! Am not real pleased. Am considering missing class due to illness.

---

11 Forgetting? Or . . . preferring not to remember?

Have just finished my first session of Strange Family 101.[12] It wasn't 100% as terrible as I expected. Mostly because we discussed absolutely no family history. Instead, Mom presented me with course materials and requirements. Am pasting in a small excerpt for reference.

History of the Strange Family
Course Syllabus

Daily, 9:00–10:00 p.m., in the living room

Welcome to the History of the Strange Family! This class will be all about your fun and fascinating ancestors, taught by your MOST fun and fascinating ancestor, PATTI STRANGE!

WEEK 1

Orientation

Overview

Guest speaker

Study questions

---

12 Mom did not believe I had contracted malaria over dinner.

That's my mom: class-A specimen of <u>Goofus spazticus.</u>

Despite her enthusiasm, I remain convinced that this class is going to be just as dry and tedious as I feared. Fingers crossed there is lots of unexpectedly juicy family gossip. My hopes are not high. Tomorrow's class will feature guest speaker Great-Aunt Millie—live (well, sort of live) from her shoe box. I guess Mom is hoping that a poltergeist guest speaker will make family history slightly less boring. We'll see about that.

Later

Just got home after roaming streets of Duntzton for a while. Not much going on. Went to the address on Said Student's ID in order to return it, but that house is vacant. Trip was not a complete loss, though. Cats and I found a loose basement window and spent a satisfying half hour poking around in the random items left behind by former tenants. Man, I LOOOOOOOVE vacant basements!

Later

Practiced Krav Maga with Raven for a while. Am very glad I happen to have a super strong, well-calibrated golem to practice martial arts with. I can fight as hard as I want with no risk of hurting her, and she is well tuned enough these days to make a really tough sparring opponent. It's kind of a shame I'm philosophically opposed to violence, because I am getting to be kind of a badass at this stuff. Trainers at Fight Club are sure to be impressed!!!!

Later

Have spent a little quality time with the old Magic 8 Ball just to get an idea of what this school year holds for me. It's a regular back-to-school ritual with me. Have been compiling school-related questions over the years. Here they are, with the 8 Ball's responses:

1. Will I be expelled this year? **Better not tell you now.**
2. Will I learn a lot? **It is decidedly so.**
3. Will I like my new teacher(s)? **Outlook good. For a change.**
4. Will my grades be good? **Like you care.**
5. Will I be in school long enough to get my desk properly booby-trapped? **Concentrate and ask again.**
6. Will I be forced to resort to threats of violence to protect myself from fearsome bullies? **Signs point to yes.**
7. Will I make enemies among the school administration? **Don't get your hopes up.**
8. Will I craft a Me-Golem who can attend classes in my

place? **Not flabbering likely!**

9. Will I need to invent a new disease to avoid finishing out the school year? **My sources say no.**

10. Will I spend much time in detention? **As if!**

11. Am I gonna find a substitute for black rock? **That question has nothing to do with school. Ask again later.**

12. Will History of the Strange Family destroy me with boredom? **Cannot predict now.**

13. Will Mom be the kind of teacher who accepts weird science projects as substitutes for book reports? **Don't make me laugh!!!**

Sept. 4

Today's assignments:
- Return Said Student's ID (LATE!!)—3 points
- Make copy of Mom's house key (VERY LATE!!!)—13 points
- Read selected works of Hadewijch of Antwerp—13 points
- Wrangle juicy tidbits of family gossip out of Mom and Great-Aunt Millie—113 points

Just finished second session of Strange Family 101. Tonight we began an overview of Great-Aunts Through the Ages. And, OK, it wasn't COMPLETELY dry and tedious. It turns out that every hundred years or so in the history of my family, there is an Aunt with some kind of cool talent. Great-Aunt Millie, for example: She died in 1761, but she's been able to stick around this world ever since. (Bog only knows why. Personally, I can't wait to go explore the next world when my time comes.) Anyway, she's been piecing together the family history for centuries, and has even met both of the Aunts who lived after her: Great-Aunt Lily (1777–1790) and Great-Aunt Emma (1887–1992).

Note-taking was required. Here are some highlights:

1. The earliest Aunt that Mom and Aunt Millie know about was Great-Aunt LaRue, who was born in the 660s. No, not the 1960s, the 1860s, or even the 1660s . . . the **660s**. Whew.
2. None of the Aunts was ever known to get married or have children. That's why they're the Aunts and not the Grandmas. Duh.
3. Like I said, they all had some kind of remarkable talent.

For example: Great-Aunt Emma LeStrande was able to crystallize the liquid black rock that flowed under her house in order to build and sculpt with it.

4. Great-Aunt Melisende Forestiero had the ability to communicate with the spirit world.
5. Great-Aunt Leah Ciudat was said to levitate herself and others at will.
6. Great-Aunt Camilla Underlig could call down all sorts of weather with a snap of her fingers.
7. Great-Aunt Mildred Különös spoke the secret languages of animals, plants, and even minerals.
8. Great-Aunt Amelia Merwürdig painted incredible portraits of people that revealed their future.
9. Great-Aunt Eleda Märklig made transcendent music on instruments she crafted of seed husks and petals.
10. And Great-Aunt Lily Étrange was known to heal animals and people of whatever ailed them.
11. As far as anyone knows, there has only been one Great-Aunt alive at any one time.
12. But it's not necessarily true that there is always one living. Mom does not know of one alive today.
13. Most of the Aunts have lived to be very old— usually over 90, and often over 100—with the exception of Great-Aunt Lily, who died of white fever when she was only 13.

So yeah. I guess the family history's not totally without interest. I mean, I definitely wouldn't mind hearing more about that levitation trick of Great-Aunt Leah's. Or Great-Aunt Emma's black rock, and where I can get some more. Oh wait, scratch that. I know exactly where to get more: back at Great-Aunt Emma's old house in Blackrock! Hmm. Road trip may be in order. Hey—call it a field trip, write a report on my experience, and I have the makings of some extra credit here.

Later

Have blown off homework and spent some glorious hours bumming around Duntzton by night. Tested my newly crafted tranquilizer blowgun on a few of the neighborhood dogs.

Brilliant!!!! From now on, canines all over town will be enjoying sweet dreams while the felines and I explore their backyards in peace. Nothing of note so far in those backyards, I'm sorry to report, but that doesn't make it any less rewarding.

Later—back at home

Sun almost up. Real pooped. Going to sleep.

Sept. 5

Today's assignments:
- Exercise 23 in Theory of Complex Numbers—13 points
- Return Said Student's ID (VERY LATE!!)—3 points
- Make copy of Mom's house key (EXTREMELY LATE!!!)—13 points
- Fingerpaint portraits of Raven, the Oddisee, and other major inventions—13 points each
- Complete Mom's study questions on Great-Aunts Through the Ages—13 points

Have spent the hours between dinner and Strange 101 doing nothing but homework. Man. Had I realized homeschooling myself was going to cut this deeply into my nighttime-bumming-around-town routine, I would not have scheduled such a heavy course load. May have to take an incomplete in Fingerpainting this semester. Ahahahhhahaaahahhhaha.

History of the Strange Family

4/5

1. Choose one Great-Aunt and describe what you
   would do if you had her special talent.

Great-Aunt Eleda—if I had her skills, I'd be rocking out to some serious Heavy Petal. Owww!

2. If Great-Aunt Amelia were to paint your portrait, what might it reveal?

Hey, Patti, is this your sly way of encouraging me to reflect on my long-term goals? NICE TRY!

3. If you could pick one Great-Aunt to have a conversation with, who would it be, and why?

Great-Aunt Millie, of course, because ~~she's reading this over my shoulder, and I have no desire to offend the family poltergeist~~ she's obviously the most interesting dead Great-Aunt a girl could have! . . . . What is this, a trick question?

4. If you had an amazing talent of your own, what
   would you like it to be?

Oh, so you don't think I'm chock-full of amazing talents, huh? If I could manage to build even half the amazing inventions that are floating around in my mind, I'd be thrilled. Alternatively, I wouldn't mind being 13 miles tall. Tokyo better look out, though!!!

Why did Great-Aunt Lily die of white fever, when she could supposedly heal people?

Later

OK—I'll admit it: Strange 101 has gotten more interesting. Great-
Aunt Millie taught class again tonight. Possibly due to the study
question I wrote, she talked mostly about Great-Aunt Lily. Not
too much is known about her—Aunt Millie saw her only once.
She lived her entire short life on the East Coast, in a small seaside
town called Seasidetown, along with her mother, Pearl, and her
sister, Opal. As we know, Lily's unusual talent was healing.[13]
And she died in an epidemic of white fever that wiped out a third
of her town's population. After that, Pearl and Opal moved to
Salem, Massachusetts, where Opal married and raised her family.

I would have left it at that if Great-Aunt Millie had just
addressed my study question in the first place, but ten o'clock
rolled around and I still hadn't gotten an answer. Mom was yawn-
ing and getting cranky, so she went off to bed while Great-Aunt
Millie and I wrapped things up.

ME: [Raising my hand like a good little pupil. Despite
    being the only pupil in the room.] Great-Aunt

---

13 Sort of a goody-goody talent, if you ask me, but impressive
nonetheless.

Millie? I don't think we've discussed my study question.

GREAT-AUNT MILLIE: [Looking uncomfortable.] Ssssorrrry, my dearrrr, what wasssss yourrrrr quesssssstion againnnnn?

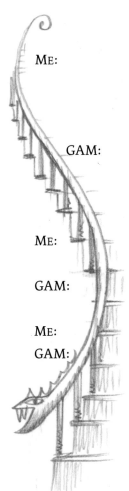

ME: Why did Great-Aunt Lily die of white fever, when she could supposedly heal people? Seriously, don't you think that's kind of odd?

GAM: [Looking even more uncomfortable.] Welll, yessssssss, my dearrrr, that hassss neverrrrr made sensssse to meeeee eitherrrrr.

ME: Weren't you around? At least in spirit?

GAM: Ohhhhhh noooooooooo, I was in Reeeeeno.

ME: You . . . were . . . in . . . Reno.

GAM: Welllll, it wassssn't Reeeno yet, but yesss, Cousin Pauliiiine had a rannnch out there in Nevaaada at that timmme. Of courrrrse, it wassssssn't Nevaaada yet, eitherrrrr. Maybeeee next weeeeek I'll give a lesssson on the Cousins. They're so much more . . . colllllllllor-fullllll . . . than the Auntssss.

28

ME: Really.

GAM: Youuuu won't belieeeeve the storieees I can tellllll about Cousin Billieeeee and her honky-tonk giraffffffe circusssss!

ME: Aunt Millie, you're not changing the subject, are you?

GAM: Cerrrrtainly not. We were discussssssssing Reeeno, I belieeeeve?

ME: No, we were discussing how SUSPICIOUS it is that Great-Aunt Lily died of white fever! Don't you think so?

GAM: Yesss . . . yesssss, it is suspiciousss.

ME: All right! Now, look, Aunt Millie, let's be honest with each other. I'm not the world's dumbest kid, and you're not the world's smoothest liar. Are you keeping something from me? Because you should know by now, that's only going to make me more interested in finding out.

GAM: Oh noooo, dearrr. Youuuu've hearrrrd it alllll. I've neverrrr understood why Lilllly didn't heal her-rrrself. Howeverrrr . . . I willl add thissss: Everrr since herrr death, "white feverrrr" has meant something awfulllll to the Darrrrrk Auntsssss.

ME: [Feeling a chill.] Did you say "Dark Aunts"?

GAM: [Flustered.] Ohhhhh . . . yessss. Great-Auntsssss, you callll us.

ME: But you said "Dark Aunts" like it was a title. Is there something dark about them?

GAM: Yessss . . . but this mussst be betweeeeeen you and meeeee. Your motherrrr wouldn't understand.

ME: [Getting downright intrigued. Despite myself.] No problem, Aunt Millie. And what was that about white fever? What does it mean to the Dark Aunts?

GAM: It's a metaphorrrr, my child. [Her voice dropping to a haunted whisper.] Like . . . sunsssshine burssssting into a darrrrrkened roooooom.

ME: [Shuddering.] Ugh! Yes. I understand. You don't get the blues, you get the whites.

GAM: There's just one otherrrr thinnnng I reculllll about Lily . . .

ME: What other thing?

GAM: It's only a famillllllly rumorrrr . . . most likely, compleeeeetely untrue. How could it beeeeee true?

ME: [Now dying of curiosity.] Great-Aunt Millie, please tell me. I HAVE to know!

GAM: [Silently studying me a while before she spoke.] Yes . . . after all, you are thirteeen, and this IS your historrrry. Very wellllll, then. They say it wassss another Darrrrk Aunt who caused Lily'ssss death.

ME: [Shocked. Horrified.] But why? HOW?

GAM: Nooooo onnnne knowsssss! But it'ssss only a

rumorrrr. There issssss absolutely noooooo evidence for it.

ME: Except that the OFFICIAL reason for her death is total hooey.

Later

Had to stop writing back there when Mom came into the room and interrupted us.

ME: Sup, Patti. Thought you were in bed.

MOM: I was, but then I thought of something . . . You guys still talking about Great-Aunt Lily?

ME: Yeah, and how weird it is that she wouldn't have healed her own white fever. Why? You got any ideas?

M: No, but I might have something better. You know, I've got heirlooms from a few of the Aunts, like a lock of Great-Aunt Emma's hair, that Polynesian tiki idol from Great-Aunt Amelia, and Great-Aunt Millie's collection of antique anatomy textbooks.

ME: That's nice, Patti. Now, what does that have to do with Aunt Lily?

M: Well, the heirloom I have from her is by far the weirdest.

ME: [Feeling a growing tingle of excitement.] Ooooh,

that IS better. What is it? Where is it?

M: It's a . . . well, I don't really know WHAT it is exactly.

ME: Wherewherewherewherewhere!

M: Cool your jets, you'll hyperventilate. It's in a crate in the basement. Your grandmother used to keep it in a terrarium, but it always gave me the super-creeps, so I packed it away where I didn't have to look at it.

So we went down to the basement and scrounged around among the boxes we had just moved from Silifordville. It took a while, but Mom eventually found it: a small wooden crate stenciled LILY ÉTRANGE.

Mom said she didn't care to see the fabled Heirloom again, so I took it up to my room for further investigation. I brought Aunt Millie with me to see what she thought of it.

I didn't even need a crowbar to open the crate—the wood was practically disintegrating around the rusted-out

nails. I pulled the lid off with my hands, and then—I admit it—
I'm not ashamed—I screamed bloody murder and jumped back in
a panic. Because inside was a twitching, lashing, LIVING

CAT TAIL!

When I caught my breath again, I looked over at
Aunt Millie to find out if she was seeing what
I was seeing. I eventually
found her under my
pillow.

The Heirloom!

ME:	What do you think? What is it? Is it real? Is it magic? Is it haunted?
GREAT-AUNT MILLIE:	[Sounding a little hysterical.] Ffffff! Bzzzzzzzzz! Hhhhhhrrrrrrrrrrr!
ME:	Gahhhh! Aunt Millie! Help me out, here. What is this thing?
GAM:	Sssssssssssmmm! Eeesssssnnnnnn- nnnlllllll? Oooozzzzzzuuuunnnnnn nnnnnnn . . .
ME:	[Sighing.] OK, you're overstimulated, let's get you back in your shoe box for the night. We'll try this again tomorrow.

Later

Further observations on the creepy cat tail: It does not appear to be mechanical. It seems to behave just as it would if still attached to

a cat. Sabbath, Miles, and NeeChee all hissed and ran at the sight of it, but Mystery seems strangely attracted to it. She picked it up out of the crate and hopped up on my bed, and is now snuggled up with the gross little thing, grooming it and purring. Ugh! I may need to sleep in the hammock tonight.

POP QUIZ!

1. Severed body parts sometimes continue to move after being detached, due to:
   a) galvanic energy
   b) gamma rays from Planet X
   c) voodoo

2. The Heirloom proves that Great-Aunt Lily was a:
   a) cat person
   b) cat-tail amputator
   c) cat

3. Great-Aunt Lily's death was most likely caused
   by:
   a) gamma rays from Planet X
   b) accidentally reverse-healing herself
   c) whoever or whatever cut the tail off her cat

Later

Cannot stop thinking about the mystery of Lily's death. I really don't see how it could have been white fever. But how could a Dark Aunt have killed her? And why???? Now that I have a relic from Lily's time, I am very tempted to use it in my Time-Out Machine and see if I can solve these mysteries.[14] And yet . . . I hesitate to just zap myself merrily into the eighteenth century. For one thing, I can't predict EXACTLY what time (or location) this cat tail will take me to. Partly because I know nothing specific about the cat tail itself, but also because I haven't EXACTLY perfected how the T.O.M. targets your destination. The theory is totally sound, but the mechanism hasn't proven to be as reliable in practice as I'd hoped.

I still think I did a pretty great job in designing the controls, based on the concept that every little thing has a unique identity. A pebble, a page torn out of a calendar, a severed cat tail, you name it. And every unique identity has a unique path in space and time. So, I just load in the object, and spin the dial to specify

---

14 Assuming I can get the flammerbarking thing running!

where along its space-time line I want to go. I've gotten pretty good at the fine-tuning. "Pretty good"—not "kick-ass." When the object is something short-lived, like a flower or a bee, then it's no big deal, but throw a dinosaur bone in there, and then you're playing with a VERY large span of time, and it gets much harder to narrow down where and when you'll end up. Even THAT wouldn't be a big problem if I were well stocked on black rock, cuz I could just keep rolling that dial, moving back and forth in time, until I found the perfect moment. However, I'm NOT well stocked on black rock right now. SIGH.

Will double-check the lab for any remaining black rock supplies tomorrow. Daylight is almost here and I am beat.

Sept. 6

Today's assignments:
- Read pages 1–343 in Particle Physics: Not for Dummies
- Practice elbow strike and hammerfist—13 points
- Return Said Student's ID (EXTREMELY LATE!!!)—3 points
- Make copy of Mom's house key (SEVERELY LATE!!!!) —13 points
- Read selected poems from Shinkokinshu—13 points
- Locate supplies of black rock—6666 points

Am determined to do a better job today of crossing assignments off my list. To that end, have dropped Said Student's ID in the nearest mailbox and simply crossed "Make copy of Mom's house key" off my list. What do I need with a house key anyway? No door or window in this house can keep me out.

Excellent progress. Am moving on.

Later

Just as I suspected—I cannot find a single drop of liquid black rock anywhere. The big jar I brought home from my trip to Great-Aunt Emma's house in Blackrock is bone-dry. Ditto every single test tube and beaker in my lab. Must have been that time I filled the kiddie pool with the stuff in order to rejoin the severed halves of my personality . . . yeah. Well, that leaves just one option. Am going to have to skip Strange 101 tonight and drive out to Blackrock. Extra credit, here I come.

Later

Mom packed us a picnic basket and gave me my assignment for the trip,[15] and now the cats and Raven and I are on the road. Good times!

Later

Vattering muckfrogs, this is very strange. Raven and I are here at the exact mile marker where Blackrock should be,

---

15 Expository essay on my journey—13 points. Extra credit for drawings and/or photos.

and . . . I don't know. There is no Blackrock here.

Have read and re-read the directions many times. I just don't understand it. Not much I can do about it now, though. I guess we'll just eat our picnic and head back home.

Spy—Cam view
of the Strangemobile!

Later

Odd stuff is going down. . . .

I was sitting cross-legged in the dust a few yards away from the van, munching a sandwich, when Raven honked the horn. I turned and looked to see her pointing into the distance. "Bag it all," she seemed to be saying. I couldn't really see anything except a cloud of dust. I walked back to the van and got her to roll the window down. "What are you saying? Bag it all? Cat is full? Pack the call?"

"ATTIKOL," she said, and my heart went cold.

Well, cold-ISH. I mean, Attikol is TECHNICALLY my ancestral enemy, and if he ever got his hands on the liquid black rock, that would be bad news. The thing is, he's not really all that bright. In fact, as far as I know, he has no clue that I'm his ancestral enemy, or what black rock is. And I need to keep it that way.

He does happen to have some tough (if excessively well-dressed) henchmen working for him. Not to mention Jakey—that kid is psychic enough to read pretty much everything that's in your head at a glance. But the henchmen don't think for themselves, and the kid and I are kind of buds, and on top of all THAT, Attikol has a terrible crush on my golem. . . . Still, I'm a little worried about what he's doing out here. Last I saw him, Raven had banished him from Blackrock for all time.

What is bringing him back again?

Let's hope it's something innocent and dumb, like, he just sort of forgot about the banishing. Not something sinister and threatening, like, he now suspects that Blackrock is hiding the source of his ancestral power.

His caravan should be here in a few minutes. Have decided fleeing the scene is not the best plan, since they may have already seen us. Also, would very much like to know what the hamcakes they are doing here. Am settling down to wait.

39

Later

Am back in the van, headed home, and trying to get a grip on what has happened.

Here's what has happened:

The caravan arrived. Raven was outside, ready to greet them. I was hunkered down in the van with the cats, not sure if it was a good idea for me to come out, hoping Jakey would signal me somehow. I watched through a peephole as the trailers pulled up; people started getting out, stretching their legs, looking around at what used to be a small town and was now just dust and dust and dust. In a few minutes, Attikol came forward and approached Raven. There was some conversation that I couldn't hear. I didn't see Jakey anywhere . . . if he wasn't here, what was I going to do? Stay hidden and hope that Raven would be able to extricate herself without my help?

"Jakey," I whispered, hoping he was close enough already to sense my thoughts. "I'm in the van. Can you—"

Then I saw the eyeball.

The eyeball slowly backed up until I could see the rest of Jakey's face, smiling at me. WHEW!!!!! I opened the van door and hopped out.

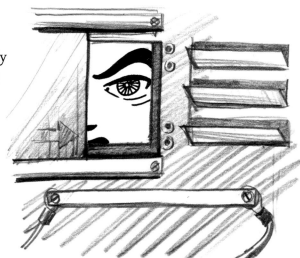

ME: Dude. You look terrible.

JAKEY: Nice to see you too.

ME: Seriously, what happened to you?

J: Oh, well, it's a long story—there was this ancient diary, and one thing led to another, and Attikol's thugs ended up holding me

My ancestral enemy and his caravan!

down and shaving my head to see if I happened to have a birthmark shaped like a moon under my hair . . .

ME: Oh, huh. Gabfrax, that thing is huge.

J: Yeah, well, turns out, there IS a reason I'm called the Moon Child.

ME: What are you guys doing here? I mean, Raven cold banished Attikol from this place, last I heard.

J: It's all about this diary he found. Hey, let's go sneak into his trailer and I'll show it to you. You're gonna flip.

ME: But . . . wait. I mean, what are the odds we would be here at the same time? I'm flipping over THAT right now.

J: Oh, that's nothing, I knew you were headed here, so I suggested it.

ME: You . . . but . . . that's not cool! I need Attikol to keep out of my family secrets, man!

J: There's nothing here for him to see. A big old dust bowl. Dust tray. Dust serving platter.

ME: Well now. Don't you think he'll find that kind of suspicious? Start asking questions? Questions that might just lead him to ME?

J: Oh. I didn't see it like that.

ME: I thought you could read ALL my thoughts.

J: Well, I guess you hadn't thought that particular thought yet.

ME: [Dry like the sandpaper.] Oh, right. You are correct. While we were driving over here, I never ONCE considered the possibility that everything might have vanished into thin air. Clearly, I am a fool.

J: OK, well, sorry about that. I really needed to talk to you, so I just told Attikol we should come out here.

ME: May I suggest that next time you just use the phone?

J: Look, come check out this diary and you'll understand.

So we snuck around to Attikol's trailer. Raven was working her magic[16] on him, and on his henchmen, so no one noticed us slipping inside.

The diary is extremely old and falling apart. Have taken a careful look at it and quizzed Jakey a bit and here is what I have learned:

1. Attikol inherited the diary along with a bunch of other family stuff when his father died a few months ago.

2. It was written by some ancestor of Attikol's named Boris, who lived on the East Coast during the late 1700s.

3. There are many similarities between Attikol and Boris: Boris also traveled with a big group of henchmen, ran a medicine show of dubious authenticity, and, to be blunt, used the vast family wealth to be a total jerkwad.

4. Of particular note to Attikol was Boris's description of his hired psychic, a young man named Caleb, who had a large moon-shaped birthmark on his scalp. Hence the forcible shaving of Jakey.

5. On August 4, 1790, Boris writes, he visited some relatives in Seasidetown. While there, his dog tangled with their cat and wounded it in the fight. (Man . . . if I didn't already dislike Boris, that was the clincher.) Later that day, he happened to witness his young relative Lily healing

---

16 Not, like, witty banter or anything. More like vacant stares in his general direction, breathing, and the occasional "Uhhhhhh . . . Iono?"

the cat using a "dark elixir" that seemed to be fountaining up from under her house.

6. Guessing (correctly) that the dark elixir was some kind of cure-all, Boris hit upon the plan of bottling this elixir and selling it to the townspeople, who were being decimated by a white fever epidemic. Not that he had any desire to help people, mind you; he just wanted to take their money and boost his reputation.

7. So he locked Lily and her family in the upstairs rooms of their home, guarded by his henchmen, while he set up bottling operations in their basement.

8. The potion worked amazingly well on seemingly any ailment—including the dread white fever. Word got around fast, and Boris sold out almost immediately.

9. But on August 6, the basement fountain dried up. Boris suspected that someone in the family was responsible.

10. He used "persuasive techniques" on them to encourage them to tell him the fountain's secrets in hopes that he could get it flowing again, but no one would help him.

11. And on August 14, young Lily was stricken with white fever and died.

12. Her mother and sister escaped Seasidetown, along with the psychic Caleb, during Lily's funeral. Boris speculated in his diary that Caleb likely sheltered them at his parents' ranch near Salem.

13. On the final page of the diary, Boris describes how he left town that night, as did everyone else who could ride, walk, or crawl away from Seasidetown and its deadly plague.

So, yeah. That's some of what I'm trying to digest right now. I mean, dark elixir?! Flowing under her house?!?! That's just a little too much like Great-Aunt Emma's black rock to be a coincidence, I think. But it gets better . . .

ME: OK, this is creepy. I never knew about Lily until two days ago, and then I meet up with you guys, and you have this diary that's all about her death?

JAKEY: Well, we've had the diary for a while. I didn't know

she was your relative until you had your first session of Strange 101.

ME: Um . . . but . . . so . . . I mean, you haven't been in Duntzton lately, right? I thought you had to be pretty close to someone to read their mind.

J: I'm getting better at it. I can read my mom's mind from across the country now.

ME: Wow . . . doesn't that drive you crazy, hearing all those people's thoughts?

J: Well, it's not like I hear everyone between me and her.

ME: So it's more selective now?

J: Yeah, I can direct it a lot more these days. Peek in on the important people . . . [Obviously reading my thoughts.] Yeah . . . sorry. I've been checking in on you. Only now and then, I swear.

ME: Uh . . . you do realize this is giving me the super-creeps, right?

J: [Looking embarrassed.] If it makes you feel any better, only the sort of big and dramatic stuff comes through from that distance. I mean, like, Great-Aunt Lily, but not, like, what you had for dinner.

ME: OK . . . well, don't make a habit of it. I need my secrets, you know.

47

That's all I said out loud, anyway. He knows as well as I do that I am trusting him not to give away my secrets to Attikol. Trusting him because I have very little choice. Trusting him when it doesn't come naturally to me to trust anyone. When I realize that the main factors keeping his mouth closed are A) his dislike for Attikol, and B) his loyalty to me. Loyalty that is somewhat based on his expectation that I will someday manage to rescue him from Attikol. An expectation that I'm not completely sure I can fulfill.

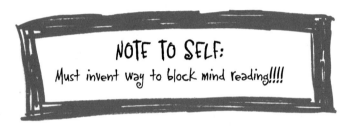

NOTE TO SELF:
Must invent way to block mind reading!!!!

ME: [Sighing. Not liking the situation any.] OK, kid, here's what I really need to know. What does this diary mean to Attikol? What does he think he's going to do with this information?

JAKEY: Oh, he thinks I'm going to betray him somehow and escape, like Caleb did to Boris.

ME: Yeah. We should be so lucky. What's he doing about it?

J: Oh, y'know, constant surveillance while we're in towns, keeping me locked up in my trailer, enforced head-shaving, threats of violence . . .

ME: Cramjams, that sucks rocks. What else?

J: Well . . . you're not going to like this.

ME: Spill it, you!

J: OK. First, he believes that the dark elixir really belongs to HIS family.

ME: Even though it was obviously Boris stealing it from Lily?

J: Yeah, well, you know he's not the smartest guy. But also, he seems to think Lily's side of the family stole it from Boris's side originally. Like, a long long time ago.

ME: OK. What else?

J: And . . . now he wants to track down the descendants of Lily's family, to see what they know about the elixir.

ME: Oh flamjars. Do you think he has a chance?

J: Uh . . . he knows your grandmother's name now. Not your mom's yet, but it's probably just a matter of time.

ME: [Gulping.] And what does he think he's going to do if he finds these descendants?

J: [Uncomfortably.] You really don't want to know the details.

ME: "Persuasive techniques," huh?

J: Yeah. I am WAY too young to be seeing some of the

stuff I've seen in that guy's mind.

ME: OK. Thanks for the warning. I'll get back to ya soon, kid.

Later

Home again. Have questioned Great-Aunt Millie on where Blackrock might have gone. Here's how THAT went:

ME: Hey, Aunt Millie, we gotta talk. Raven and I just drove out to Aunt Emma's old house in Blackrock . . . I mean we <u>tried</u>. There was nothing there! Mile marker 923, right? Did we go to the right spot?

GREAT-AUNT MILLIE: Youuuu were in the same sssspot where you found it lasssst, yesssssss.

ME: All right, so . . . where was Blackrock?

GAM: My dearrrr, Blackrock isss not a physsssical place, tied to physsssical coorrrrdinates. When Emma died, Blackrock began to lose itsssss anchorrrrr in this worlllld. And when youuuu left, it came unmoorrrrrred in space-tiiiimme.

ME: [Sighing] Gahhh. So how can I find it again?

50

GAM:	You mayyyy never find it againnn.
ME:	[Trying to swallow my incredible disappoint-ment.] OK. Anything you advise?
GAM:	[Long pause.] If you'rrrrre meant to find it, then onnnnnne day you willllll find it . . . but no one can helllllp you with that but yoursssssself.

This is terrible. Unbelievable. I have totally squandered my inheritance from Great-Aunt Emma!!!!! If I had only known Blackrock was going to disappear like this, I would have brought way more black rock home with me, never wasted it on silly uses (e.g., fingerpaint, axle grease, shampoo), and/ or never left Blackrock to begin with!

Black Rock from Blackroc

REFILL

POP QUIZ!

1. Great-Aunt Lily's dark elixir was actually:
    a) crude oil
    b) black cherry soda
    c) liquid black rock

2. (Revised) Great-Aunt Lily's death was most likely
   caused by:
   a) Boris' "persuasive techniques"
   b) white fever
   c) being shut away from her healing dark elixir
      when she got white fever
   d) all of the above

3. The worst part of all this is that:
   a) Jakey is reading my mind at great distances
   b) Attikol and I are BOTH on the hunt for
      liquid black rock
   c) Attikol's ancestors and mine appear to have
      been relatives[17]

4. If I could just get myself back to 1790, I might
   be able to:
   a) help Aunt Lily get rid of Boris
   b) save her life
   c) use her dark elixir to get myself home[18]
   d) change the past somehow in order to prevent
      Attikol from ever tracking down the
      descendants of Aunt Lily's family

---

17 Ewwwwwwwwwwwwwww.
18 And I wouldn't mind a little extra supply to use in experiments.

Sept. 7

Today's assignments:
- Practice standard tunings for the guitar—13 points
- Avoid dying of boredom while practicing standard tunings for the guitar—53 points
- Invent way to block mind reading—113 points
- Get T.O.M. running and save Aunt Lily's life— 13 million points

Have been doing some research on The Mind in hopes of finding a workable way to keep Jakey from reading mine. Have rejected the idea of giving myself total amnesia. Not that it wouldn't work (been there, done that). No, I'm looking for something more selective. I don't really need to block Jakey from everything in my mind (e.g., it will be nice for him to know immediately when I beat his high score at Brats Blow Chunks), but I would like to keep certain family secrets and other intellectual property from him.[19] All I'm asking for is a kind of mental barrier. A brain partition, if you will.

Disappointingly, most of the literature on psychic power is either A) obviously written from the point of view that psychic power is a fairy tale, B) intended for IQs in the double digits, or C) in Russian. What I need is some solid scientific research on the topic. Clearly, most reputable scientists have shied away from

---

19 Approx. 99.66% of my thoughts.

having their names associated with investigation of psychic power. Too bad!!!! Will keep trying.

Later

Have done an exhausting amount of reading and come up with two possible solutions: dissociative identity disorder and self-hypnosis. After a LOT of thought, have finally decided that dissociative identity disorder simply will not do. Granted, having multiple personalities in my head would no doubt be interesting and novel. I mean, of course I've done the whole dividing-my-personality-into-two-warring-bodies bit, and THAT was certainly a wild ride. To say the least. But when it comes down to it, I think I'd rather just be alone. That leaves me with self-hypnosis, which has a much better chance of working with fewer disastrous side effects (e.g., no interminable hours of therapy, no hospitalization, no The Three Faces of Emily).

Later

Self-hypnosis is EXCELLENT!!!!!!! Have practiced a bit and performed a quick experiment, which consisted of concealing a test phrase ("BRICKLEBITING FRICKLETS") in my mind, then calling up Jakey. Spent a few minutes chatting with him about random topics, then casually asked if he could tell me the test phrase. Much to his irritation, he could not. YESSSSS!!!

Me: Look, I'm gonna try going back to Lily and Boris'
         time to see what I can do about all this. I don't
         suppose you could still read my mind if I were
         visiting the past, huh?

Jakey: Uh, probably not.

Me: Even bet—I mean, too bad. Hey, I'll call ya later,
         kid. Hang in there.

Later

Have taken apart the Oddisee and transferred the PPC® into
the Time-Out Machine. Then scraped together all the dried
flakes of black rock I could find. I had to reinflate my kiddie
pool and dismantle several very nicely-built contraptions to get
a few more precious grains. I have absolutely no idea if dried
black rock will even do the trick, and there is nowhere near
enough of it for any testing or fine-tuning. Fingers AND
toes crossed that my first jump back is on target. I
think that in this case, I have a VERY good chance
of my targeting being pretty exact. I mean, I now
know the actual date the cat tail was severed. Should
be no big deal to dial in to any spot on its time line that
I choose.

Assuming the T.O.M. works at all, that is.

Am looking around my room at the mess I've made trying to get the T.O.M. up and running. Wondering if it is even
worth the effort. I really should bear in mind

that the further back in time I go, the more dangerous it will be for me there. I could come down with white fever, or smallpox, or rabies, or . . . the vapors, or some other hideous disease I have no resistance to. Or, I could be burned at the stake as a witch! Uh . . . actually, am pretty sure they were not still killing witches in the 1790s. And let's be honest, I am perfectly capable of whipping up a batch of white fever vaccine, or any other vaccine, in my home lab. Should really start considering the pros of going back instead of focusing on the cons.

Later

I think it IS worth the effort to go back. I mean, if all I do is keep Lily from dying of white fever at age 13, I'll feel like I accomplished something. But it's not just that. If this trip goes well, I have a chance to keep Attikol off my trail. And that's pretty huge.

Plus . . . Lily had her own fountain of dark elixir/liquid black rock. Is it too much to think she might be able to tell me how to find Blackrock again?

Later

Have made some preparations:
1. Whipped up batch of white fever vaccine.
2. Vaccinated myself and packed doses for Lily and family.
3. Attempted to get the creepy cat tail away from Mystery. No dice! She ran into the basement with it and refused to come out, even for snack treats.

4. Wrote Mom a note that went a little something like this: "Yo Patti—Have gone back in time to vaccinate Great-Aunt Lily. Will hopefully return before you read this note. If you ARE reading this note, it probably means I screwed up the space-time continuum. If I did THAT, then most likely, neither of us was ever born. Therefore, you are not reading this note. See ya soon—E."

5. Threw the note away.

6. Gave Sabbath, NeeChee, and Miles lots of extra cuddles, snuggles, babytalks, and snack treats, in case I fail to be born.

7. Attempted some research on 1790s fashions in case I need to disguise myself. I will not be wearing any of those clothes, I tell you that. Will just have to travel by cover of dark.

8. Tried again to get Mystery out of the basement. She eventually ran into the attic with the cat tail. Slagtix!!!!!

9. After much thought, decided to tune the Time-Out Machine to take me to August 5—the day after the cat tail was severed from the cat, when Lily was already confined upstairs. This should prevent me from encountering Boris unexpectedly, but get me there before the dark elixir dries

up. Cannot afford to take any chances getting back home!!!

10. Snagged an apple off neighbor's tree to take with me, so I can be sure to get back to my own time.

11. Switched Raven into downtime mode to prevent any unanticipated mischief. Much better to have her sitting around with her mouth open until I return.

12. FINALLY managed to corner Mystery in my room with the blasted cat tail. Now if I can just get it away from her for a moment!

13. Booby-trapped bedroom door and windows, just in case of intruders. You never know!

Later

This is not fun. Have been chasing Mystery around my room for the past half hour. Mystery thinks this is all the most glorious jamboree of good times and glee. I, on the other hand, am making up new swearwords at a rate of 3 per second. GABBERPLUCKING FELINE!!!!

~~LATER~~ EARLIER!!!!!!!!!!!!!
Like, 200+ years earlier!!!!!

IT WORKED!!!!!! AM BACK WITH LILY!!!!!!!!!!!! AM SO EXCITED!!!!!!!!!!!!!

OK. Must settle down and describe events from the beginning.

IT WORKED IT WORKED IT WORKED

Great-Aunt Lily!

I finally got the tail away from Mystery for a moment and stuck it in the Time-Out Machine. OF COURSE, just as I was pressing the GO button, Mystery leaped inside and grabbed hold of the tail. What did I expect her to do? Well, so she's here with me now, hanging out with Lily's (tail-free) cat, Enigma. But more on that later.

So yeah. Pressed the GO button. Everything winked away from around me and for a weird, timeless, endless instant, I was floating in Nothing, in X-space and X-time, in darkness that wasn't dark, because to be dark is to be SOMETHING; then we were there in Lily's bedroom, watching Lily put a severed (but still wiggling) cat tail into a small wooden crate stenciled LILY ÉTRANGE.

She didn't see me yet. I thought I should probably alert her that I was there before she started, I don't know, picking her nose or something.

ME: Hey, Lily, don't freak out, I'm your, uh, cous—

LILY: AIIIIIEEEEEEEEEE!!!!!

ME: Shh, shh, seriously, everything's OK. I'm a relative of yours. I'm here to help you.

L: [Backed against the wall. Staring wildly at the Time-Out Machine. Looking very freaked out.] How did you get in here?

ME: Long story. I came from the future. I'm here to vaccinate you against white fever.

L: Who ARE you?

ME: I'm your, hm, well, actually I'm like your Great-Great-Great-Great-Niece, only with about ten "greats" in there. But you can call me Cousin Emily. All I want to do is vaccinate you, OK?

L: What does "vaccinate" mean?

ME: Oh, you know . . . oh. Right. You don't know. Vaccines aren't gonna be invented for another six years. Well, it's like a medicine you take before you get sick.

L: [Silently blinking at me in fear and shock.]

ME: [Jovially.] Well, no time like the present! Er, the past! Whatever! C'mon . . . [Taking syringe out of my pocket and approaching her with it.] What do you say we get this stuff in your vein, now-ish? No telling when you might come down with something deadly.

L:	[Staring in terror at me and the fairly horrific needle I was pointing at her.] AIIIEIIIEIIEEEE!!!!!!
VOICE FROM OTHER ROOM:	Lily? Are you well?
ME:	[Hoping I sounded like Lily.] Yes . . . very well . . . thank you! [To Lily.] Seriously, Lily, listen up. You know this dude Boris? Bad guy? He's been stealing your dark elixir?

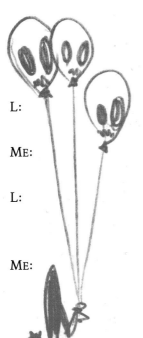

L:	[Obviously trying to get hysteria under control.] Yes?
ME:	I'm here to help you out with that, so pull yourself together, OK?
L:	[Struggling . . . obviously struggling.] What does that mean . . . "OK"?
ME:	[Slapping self on forehead for not doing more research on 1790s colloquialisms.] It means "all right." And I'm your friend. I'm your RELATIVE. Hey, look at us! Don't tell me you can't see the family resemblance! Hey . . . look at our CATS!
L:	[Staring at our two black cats, who

were ecstatically grooming each other and making a combined noise like twenty-three hives of
bees in a motorboat.] Yes . . . that IS odd. Enigma
doesn't usually like other felines.

ME: Yeah, there we go. Let's just sit down here at the . . .
er, sideboard . . . thingy . . . and have a cup of tea,
or something, and get to know each other a little,
what do you say?

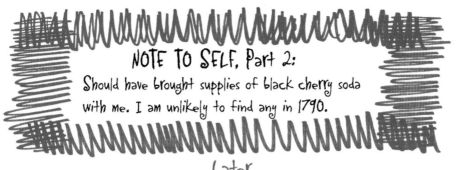

NOTE TO SELF, Part 2:

Should have brought supplies of black cherry soda with me. I am unlikely to find any in 1790.

Later

HORRIBLE NEWS!!!!!!!!

It's not August 5 . . . it's AUGUST 7.

Despite my best efforts to get here the day after the tail was severed, and before the fountain of dark elixir dried up, I have arrived too late.

There is no black rock here.

My Time-Out Machine is useless.

I AM STUCK IN THE 1790s!!!!!!!!!!!!!!!!

Here's how I found out: Lily and I were sitting at the sideboard thingy, enjoying our little vaccination/teatime chat, when it occurred to me that I had better secure some of her dark elixir sooner than later.

ME: Hey, Lily, I understand you have a dark elixir that you use to heal people?

LILY: [Looking suddenly wary.] Yessss . . .

ME: I used to have some of that stuff myself. I call it black rock. I got it from another one of my Dark Aunts . . . who won't actually be born for another hundred years or so. Anyway, I've been using it to power my inventions. Y'know, like my Time-Out Machine over there. Well, here's the thing, see, I used up my remaining supplies getting back to your time and, ahem, saving your life,[20] so I was wondering . . .

L: I would gladly give you all the dark elixir you require, Cousin Emily, but I have none myself.

ME: WHA—[choking]—Nooooooo! But . . .

L: Yes, the fountain in our basement has dried up completely. I do wish I knew how to make it flow once more, for Uncle Boris will bring us no food until I do, and my family and I are ravenous.

ME: But . . . don't you have some kind of reserve supply? A big jar of it hidden away in a closet somewhere? Something?!??!???!

L: I have nothing.

In a panic, I sprinted to the Time-Out Machine. Looked in the hopper to see if any specks of dried black rock remained so I could roll back one precious day. ALL GONE!!!! I must have run out just before I got to August 5. Oh if only I had managed to

---

20 Well, at least I've changed THIS version of history enough that she won't be dying of white fever. I suppose she could still die of scurvy, "persuasive techniques," or gamma rays from Planet X.

scrape up a few more precious grains!

Am dying a little inside right now. I am stranded in a time 100 years before the lightbulb. 150 years before the skateboard. 200 years before the Chia Pet. Am feeling insanely claustrophobic and **FREAKED OUT!!!!!** Must calm down. Must THINK. Must . . . AaaaaIIIIEeeeE! Am not calm AT ALL!!!!!

Later

Had to stop writing back there and do some meditation in the vulture pose for a while until I got a grip on myself. Am calmer, but very, very worried about my chances of returning to my own time. I see now that it was incredibly careless of me to just blithely zap myself into the 1790s without making FLATHERING CERTAIN that I had a way home.

Would compose Note to Self about properly cautious future use of the T.O.M., except I don't think I will ever get the chance to use that advice.

Later

Have been talking with Lily in hopes of learning something useful and/or taking my mind off the fact that I will likely never return to my own time. Here are some high points of our conversation:

1. Boris IS her relative. Third cousin thrice removed, but still. Grrrrrrr!
2. As I know from his diary, he got here three days ago with

his traveling medicine show.

3. The day he arrived, his dogbeast attacked Enigma and BIT OFF HER TAIL!

4. Lily used her dark elixir to heal the wound and save Enigma from bleeding to death, but could not reattach the tail. (Actually, she was shocked and horrified when I even suggested reattaching the tail. Had to remind myself that reattaching severed body parts was not invented until the 1960s. What a shame . . . wasted years, wasted appendages!!)

5. She couldn't bring herself to get rid of the severed tail, since it still seemed alive (possibly due to being soaked in dark elixir). It was even reflecting Enigma's moods. It was only today that she decided to box it up, as it was creeping out her mother and sister.

6. Lily agrees with me that dogs are more trouble than most animals, though admittedly nicer than most people.

7. As we know, Boris saw Lily using the dark elixir to heal Enigma. He helped himself to a bottle of it, called it Uncle Boris' Fever Reliever, and tried it out in his medicine show that very day.

8. After dozens of spectacular cures, Boris quickly did three things: A) imprisoned Lily's family in the upstairs rooms of their house and nailed shut all the windows,
B) installed a bottling operation in their basement, and

C) quadrupled the price on a bottle of Fever Reliever.

9. But after two days of being basically worshipped as a sort of magical healer from heaven, Boris discovered that the fountain of dark elixir had gone dry.

10. He ordered his henchmen to begin digging under the house to see if they could reopen the source. No luck.

11. Naturally, he tried entreating, pleading, coercing, threatening, and cajoling Lily's family to tell him the secret of the dark fountain. With no results.

12. This morning he announced that he would not be bringing the family any food until they decided to help him.

13. Lily gratefully accepted my last two licorice sticks, but then promptly went and gave them to her mother and sister.

Mystery and Enigma (with phantom tail).

OK. So. There is a small ray of hope here, IF someone somewhere in the town still has a little Fever Reliever left, and IF I can somehow locate it. I admit the chances of this are not excellent, but it's something to cling to.

On top of all that, I am already hungry, and the knowledge that there is no food in the house isn't quieting my stomach any.

Will have to bust out of here ASAP!

Have scoped the house situation. Boris' men have it pretty well surrounded, so this will be a little more difficult than just jimmying a window. Wish I had the blueprints of the house and some satellite photos of the grounds. And a basic toolkit. And some scrap lumber. And a working Time-Out Machine. SIGH.

Have asked Lily if I can meet her family, to see if they have any useful information and/or supplies. Also feel the need to get my Time-Out Machine into a secure hiding spot, but Lily assures me it is perfectly safe in her room. I bet she has some pretty good booby traps of her own.

Have met Lily's mother, Pearl, and her older sister, Opal. Lily did an excellent job of priming them for meeting me, so there were no hysterics. It seems that Pearl is a huge believer in the spirit world, so Lily simply told her that I am a relative from another time. Pearl has obviously assumed I am already dead. This is apparently less creepy to her than believing that I have not been born yet. Whatever works.

Opal is eighteen and much like her mother, i.e., very nice, and most certainly cut from

Pearl and Opal

a different cloth than Lily. To be specific: cheery, pastel, floral cloth, with plenty of ribbon and lace trimmings. What I like best about Opal right now, though, is the fact that she and Caleb (Boris' psychic) are in loooooooove, and (unbeknownst to Boris) engaged to be married. Turns out, this isn't Boris and Caleb's first visit to the Étrange family; otherwise, I might have to lecture Opal on the Dangers of Loving Too Fast. Ahahahahahaha!!— Like I care. Anyway, it's excellent news. We would be in deep

fewmets if Boris had a psychic in his loyalties as well as on his payroll. We are going to enlist Caleb in sneaking me out of the house. Plans are pending; more later.

Later

Cannot believe I am wearing what I'm wearing.

Mostly I did it to please Lily, who seemed to be enjoying herself. I do not plan on letting anyone see me. At least all her clothing is black. I cannot believe how many items of apparel these people wear at one go. Lily's basic underclothes

cover more skin than my dress! Just to hang around the house, she wears more layers than I would wear to go snowboarding. And the BONNET!!!! Let's not even talk about the bonnet. I do not see how she stands it.

POP QUIZ!

1. Regrettably, Uncle Boris is:
   a) more evil than I expected
   b) smarter than Attikol
   c) a dog person
   d) all of the above

2. My best chance of returning to my own time is:
   a) Finding Great-Aunt Millie at Cousin Pauline's ranch in Reno
   b) swiping some sick person's last few drops of Fever Reliever
   c) wishing the 1790s AWAAAAAAAY!

3. I would rather be caught wearing _____ than a bonnet.
   a) bunny ears
   b) spy diapers
   c) unwashed lederhosen

I did it! Am out of the house! Am hiding behind an empty shed, catching my breath. Here's how it went down: Opal alerted Caleb by urgent thought message that we were going to attempt an escape

and we needed him to create a diversion. He informed Boris that a group of street youths was attacking his medicine show. Boris immediately led most of his thugs into town to res-cue his caravan, leaving only two guards, one at each door. Meanwhile, Lily and I had crept into the attic via a tiny hidden trapdoor in Pearl's bedroom, then crawled along the rafters to a small window overlooking the back of the house. We'd been right—Boris hadn't bothered to nail up the attic windows!

I anchored the rope we'd made out of bedsheets

(CLASSIC!) to a rafter while Lily slid the window open. I went down the bedsheets, and Lily pulled up the rope behind me. Yes! Free at last![21]

Lily will be back at the window in two hours. Hopefully that's plenty of time for foraging. Am getting VERY hungry, and, unlike Lily and family, I've had a couple meals in the past twelve hours. Fever Reliever Recovery Effort may just have to wait!

Later

Have raided—or tried to raid—the Étrange family garden. Sure wish I were not so pressed for time. It is packed with the most amazing trees and plants, but, unfortunately, none of them look edible. Would like to sit around at my leisure sketching some of those flowers. Maybe later. I have never seen

---

21 OK, it had only been about an hour . . .
   but still, one hour of imprisonment is too long for me.

Weird Weeds

anything like some of them, and I think I'm pretty good at ID'ing odd flowers!

Later

Have raided—or tried to raid—the fruit trees in the next-door neighbors' garden. Unfortunately they have a savage dogbeast patrolling their property. Had to scrabble over the fence in a bit of a panic.[22] Will not be helping myself to their apples anytime soon.

NOTE TO SELF:
Always bring tranquilizer blowgun along on trips to the past!

OK—must get a move on and check out the food situation in town. I hope they are big on veggie sandwiches in 1790!!!!!!!!

Later

I should have known they wouldn't be big on veggie sandwiches in 1790. Also, it looks like they are not big on A) vegetarian restaurants that put perfectly good food in their Dumpsters, B) vegetarian restaurants, or C) restaurants. I could not find a single one! They probably have not been invented yet. Will have to look in the garbage cans outside the taverns and inns.

---

22 Doing minor damage to Great-Aunt Lily's clothing in the process. Girls really did not dress for physical activity in the 1790s.

Later

The "food" being tossed out of the taverns and inns of Seaside-town is not fit for the worms crawling in it. Clearly, they are not big on public health and safety in 1790.

Later

They are also not big on advertising in 1790—not compared to the load I'm used to, anyway—but I've already seen several posters for Uncle Boris' stolen dark elixir.

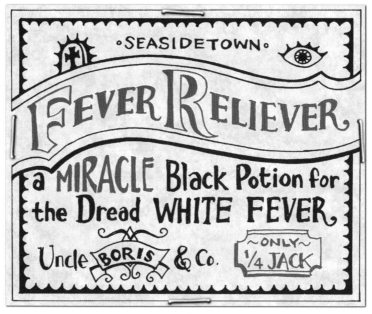

Later

My plan for not letting anyone see me dressed like this has clearly gone by the wayside. I keep expecting people to point and laugh.

Then I realize I look completely unremarkable. Cannot get used to wearing so much FABRIC.

Later

Now that I'm out and about in my 1790s gear, I can fully appreciate the functionality and genius of the bonnet: A) It is completely sunproof; B) No one can see my face; C) I don't have to see anyone else's face. Of course, for once, I WANT to see people's faces, because I'm in the fallberjocking 1790s, and everyone looks fascinatingly alien. Though I must say there are a few extremely modern-looking people in 1790. One or two could pass for hipsters from big cities, circa 1981, or even 1991 if you count some of the stablehands.

ESPrints

Later

One precious hour has gone by. Am somewhat anxious, and getting hungrier. Can only imagine how Lily, Pearl, and Opal must feel. Wish I could zap back home and hit up a grocery store, where

Why you ALWAYS bring a spy-cam and pocket printer to the 1790s!!!!

they recognize my money. Could really wow Lily with modern foodstuff novelties, like, I don't know, seedless watermelon, or Ho Hos.

Later

Am clearly desperate. I just followed a CHICKEN to her NEST behind a STABLE, where I found four eggs. Have stolen them from her, with apologies. I hope Pearl has the technology to cook them. Have also picked a bonnetful of dandelion greens. It's all I could find. Have to meet Lily at the window in five. Must run.

Later

Pearl thanked me many times for the provisions, and apologized for not offering me any money earlier. Am slapping my forehead. Should have thought to ask Lily about that.

Opal boiled our eggs in the teapot and served them sliced atop a bed of wilted greens. It was very tasty, as appetizers go. We are all still hungry. I offered to make another run, but it's getting dark, the stores are closed, and Boris' men have returned to their posts. We had to fill up on tea, and are now off to bed on semi-empty bellies. More later.

Later

Lily and I are !!wired!! from too much black tea and cannot fall asleep.[23] Instead, we are having a good old-fashioned slumber party and talking each other's ears off.[24] Here's what I have learned:

1. The dark elixir started flowing under this house on the day Lily was born. She doesn't know why it stopped or how to restart it.

2. Similarly, she has no clue how I would locate either black rock or Blackrock. Gagbax!

3. Opal was actually the one to discover the dark elixir, having been banished from the upstairs during Lily's birth. She heard meowing from the basement, and when she opened the door, she found a kitten drenched in black liquid. Enter Enigma!

4. Lily calls Enigma her best friend. With a little questioning, I was able to clarify that Enigma is also her ONLY friend.

5. Lily mentioned casually that she is not well liked by her schoolmates, who consider her to be in a perpetual state of mourning, based on the fact that she A) always wears

---

23 Would not normally be able to fall asleep at 9 p.m. anyway, but was up all day with Lily. Am finding it curious that a Dark Aunt would be awake during daylight hours. Must question Lily about this.

24 Uncharacteristically social for both of us. I blame A) caffeine, B) giddiness from lack of sleep, and C) Lily's 13-year abstinence from socializing.

black, B) rarely speaks, and C) never smiles.

6. Lily allows this misunderstanding to continue because A) her father is indeed dead, and she does indeed mourn him; B) adults expect little of her; and C) it results in slightly less tormenting from the other kids.

7. The tormenting usually takes the form of taunts and name-calling, with occasional rotting food or snakes thrown in her hair. Sometimes boys will shoot rocks at her with their slingshots.

8. When I asked Lily if she ever fought back, she seemed confused by the concept.

9. Forget about elbow strikes, hammerfisting, and groin kicks; apparently, no one has ever told her that she is capable of doing anything in life other than A) speaking when spoken to, B) keeping clean and tidy, C) the occasional healing of the sick, and D) embroidery.

10. Granted, she has some wicked embroidery skills, but this

part of the conversation kind of enraged me.

11. Was only further enraged to find out that women LOST the right to vote in Seasidetown the year Lily was born. Did not have the heart to tell her they would not get it back for another 150 years.

12. Have offered to give Lily slingshotting lessons so she can start fighting back. She was doubtful that any girl could possess the muscle power to operate a slingshot. Had to give her a demonstration before she would believe.

13. The 1790s is not the best time in history to be a girl.

Sunday, August 8, 1790

Today's assignments:
- Locate provisions—13 points
- Avoid further sunlight—13 points
- Get hands on Fever Reliever—313 points

Bellies are very insistent on getting fed today, but the back door is being guarded by a very tough-looking thug holding a musket. Opal has brainwaved Caleb that we need another henchman diversion. Lily and I are hanging out in the attic, waiting for Musket Man to step away. I have some 1790 money in my pocket. Am ready for a real grocery run.

Later

Musket Man has not budged. Lily and I are tired of the rafters. Headed downstairs to fill our bellies with tea.

ESPrint

Caleb

Later

We went into Pearl's room, where Pearl and Opal have set up their makeshift kitchen at the fireplace, to find Caleb hanging out with them. The resemblance to Jakey is pretty stunning.

Turns out he DID get Opal's message, but the timing is not good for a henchman diversion. Apparently, Boris got very suspicious yesterday when no actual street youths were found attacking his medicine show. So instead, Caleb got permission to bring us fresh water and carry away our chamber pots.[25] He was able to smuggle in some slices of bread (in a single layer inside his shirt—pretty smushed, but absolutely delicious) and some dried meat, which Lily

---

25 YES! Chamber pots. They are every bit as disgusting as I always feared.

and I left to Opal and Pearl, much to their amusement. They both seem very entertained with my similarities to Lily, though I thought it was sort of uncool for them to tease us about it in front of Caleb.

OPAL: Look how her eyes go narrow, Mother. Isn't she the very picture of our Lily?

PEARL: Yes, Dark Girls through and through, the both of them!

ME: What do you mean, Dark Girls?

LILY: [Annoyed.] I'll tell you later.

P: Why, I'll tell you now, Cousin Emily, though I'm quite surprised you don't know. Young Caleb will no doubt find this aspect of our family history diverting. Every once in a long while, as far back as our family tree is traced, there have been born Dark Girls, females of unusual talents and dark sensibilities. [To Caleb.] Perhaps this is why we are able to accept your own unusual talent without prejudice.

CALEB: I appreciate that, madam.

ME: [Strained.] Aunt Pearl, are you saying that you think I'm one of the Dark Girls?

P: A fool could see that. Why, you have Aunt Millie's eyes!

ME: [Feeling weak.] Aunt Millie . . . I know her.

P: Of course you do! She once visited me from the Beyond when Lily was young. She was never quite as . . . physical . . . a manifestation as you are, though. Quite incorporeal, Aunt Millie.

ME: [Feeling trembly and nauseated.] I feel a bit vapory actually. I think I'd better run along to Lily's room and lie down.

C: I must be off as well. My dear Miss Opal, Miss Lily, I look forward to your freedom with uplifted heart. Mrs. Étrange, I bid you adieu. Miss Emily, I shall accompany you out.

No sooner had we closed the door behind us than Young Caleb gripped my arm in a rather ungentlemanly way and stared into my eyes menacingly.

CALEB: See here, Miss Emily, I know perfectly well you are no ghost.

ME: Never said I was.

C: You do realize I can read all your thoughts, everything in your mind, as clearly as if it were written out on parchment before my eyes?

ME: Yeah, I'm familiar with the concept.

C: Then perhaps you can explain a most disturbing

thought that flashed into your mind just now in Mrs. Étrange's room.

ME: [Feeling obstinate. After all, he was gripping my arm kind of hard.] I don't know, man. I have disturbing thoughts all day long. Which one was it, exactly?

C: You believe that you will bring about Miss Lily's death.

ME: Oh, that one. I guess you also know I'm not too happy about that possibility?

C: . . . Yes.

ME: Great, how about letting go of my arm, for starters? If you don't mind, I'd kind of like to go lie down and think this over.

He let me go and went on his way, but the look in his eyes was deeply suspicious.

Later

Drat Caleb and his clabbering psychic powers!!! Drat the stupid family rumor about a Dark Aunt killing Lily!!! Drat my lack of black rock, getting me stuck here in the 1790s, possibly for a long long time!!!!! I had better get back home before I get too elderly!!!!!!

On the other hand . . . . I AM ONE OF THE DARK GIRLS!!!!!!!!!!!!!!!!!!

That's pretty dagvattering incredible.

Also . . . I think I've known it all along.

Later

Here are a few of the thoughts fighting for airtime in my mind right now:

1. I am a Dark Girl I am a Dark Girl FLAMDRAM IT ALL I am a Dark Girl AM I REALLY A DARK GIRL???????
2. Does Mom know?
3. And how EXACTLY did Aunt Pearl know? "Aunt Millie's eyes"—it's gotta be more than that!
4. Does Aunt Millie know?
5. Are Aunt Lily and Aunt Emma the only ones who had a personal fountain of liquid black rock?
6. Or is there a chance that I have one too?
7. Dark sensibilities—got 'em.
8. But what's my unusual talent?[26]
9. Am I really gonna cause Aunt Lily's death?
10. I mean, I THINK I just saved her life.
11. Maybe that family rumor got passed down wrong.
12. Yeah, that's it.
13. Am clinging to this possibility with all my heart.

---

[26] It better not be slingshotting, skateboarding, or shredding on the guitar. I mean, I'm proud of my skills, but I'll hold out for something more . . . extraordinary.

Later

Have decided to take the attitude that, while I currently have no way back to my own time, I AM a Dark Girl, and I'm hanging out with another Dark Girl, and that between the two of us, we ARE going to find a way for me to get home. In the meantime, I've shown Lily my apple and explained very, very carefully to her why it's so critical that no matter how hungry she gets, she can't eat it.[27] I asked her where we could hide it so that no one else would see it and eat it, and she just shrugged and said, "Oh, no one ever enters MY room." Have tucked it out of sight behind the Time-Out Machine so the two of us are not tempted by its beautiful color and sweet aroma.

Gragdarts. Am HUNGRY. Time for another food run soon.

Later

Back in the attic rafters with Lily, waiting for the guard to step away. Tummies are growling. Hopefully he takes a bathroom break soon.

LOTS later

Musket Man has not budged in forever and I am STARVING. Am taking matters into my own hands.

---

27 How awesome that I had to bring an off-limits tasty foodstuff
    tasty foodstuff into a house where everyone is ravenous!

Ten minutes later

I'm out! Here's how I managed it: I browsed around in the attic for a while, looking for something heavy. Finally found an old iron. It weighs approximately 2,366 times more than a modern iron. I tied it to the end of the bedsheet rope, quietly slid the attic window open, and dropped it on the guard's head, ready to pull it back up like a flash if I missed. I didn't miss. Musket Man fell over and took a nap.

Lily has promised to check for me every hour on the hour to see if I am outside needing to be let in. Am now heading to the store that Pearl recommended. Here is the shopping list she gave me:

IRON FIST

LIST

Floure
Gritts
Tea
Cyder
Hominy
Potatoes
Molasses

Am trying not to look too hard at that last iteme. ITEM. Clearly, these people have never heard of the food pyramid, let alone standardized spelling. Overall this is the oddest shopping list I have ever been given.[28]

---

28 Though nowhere near as odd as some I've written myself

86

1. What in hex is "hominy"????
   a) magic word used to summon truant kitties
      home
   b) euphemism for "ugly"
   c) part of rat

2. People ate such weird foods in the 1790s because:
   a) the Native Americans were enjoying a massive
      prank on them
   b) the invention of squid-ink pasta was still
      190 years in the future
   c) even gritts start to look tasty when you're
      hungry enough to eat dirt

Later

Have been to ye olde grocer's establishmente. Hominy is great big gross kernels of corn. Totally unappetizing. Then again, absolutely nothing on Pearl's list looks super promising to me. Am hoping she has a secret stash of licorice, black cherry jam, or veggie sandwiches somewhere in her bedroom.

Have picked another bonnetful of dandelion greens, just to be safe. Don't want anyone coming down with scurvy.

Later

Have been hunkered in the shrubbery outside Lily's house for the past half hour, watching the attic window and wondering how

Musket Man and Thugly

I'm going to get past the new guard. I arrived in time to see Musket Man getting kicked awake by his colleague, an astonishingly ugly[29] thug I like to call Thugly. Musket Man could not say what had happened to him, but did a lot of moaning about his poor poor head, and then staggered away. Nice! I hope all Boris's ruffians have this kind of work ethic.

Later

Am back indoors, thanks to Caleb. He appeared at the side of the house and stood there silently, out of sight of the guard under the window, gazing into the shrubbery until I caught his eye. Then he held up a finger as if signaling me to be patient. Sure enough, a moment later, Lily appeared at the window, and right on cue, Caleb walked around the corner, waving to the guard.

---

29 Uglier than hominy, that's for sure.

CALEB: There's something very odd floating in the cistern. I think you should have a look at it.

THUGLY: [Turning to go.] Hmmph. Blasted lazy psychic.

C: [Stage whisper.] Miss Emily, make haste!

I ran across the garden and he lifted me quickly onto his shoulders and practically launched me at the window while Lily scrambled to get it open wide enough for me and the provisions to fit through. When I was safely inside, I risked one last glance out to thank Caleb, and to satisfy a burning curiosity.

ME: By the way, what'd you put in the cistern?

CALEB: I'd rather not say . . . it's not fit for a lady's ears. But never fear, I'll be bringing your drinking water from a clean source!

Later

I take back all I said about hominy, gritts, moleasses, and the rest. Pearl and Opal are culinary geniuses. Our stomachs are delightfully full and we are all very cheerful. (Pearl and Opal are mostly cheerful due to the cyder. That stuff smells like jet fuel!!!! Am sticking with tea.)

Unfortunately there is absolutely nothing to feed Mystery. I had to tell her that, like Enigma, she is on her own for meals. Luckily, like Enigma, she is a wicked hunter, and Lily's house is full of vermin. Do not like Mystery eating vermin, though. Must get back to my own time, and its high-quality organic kibble, before much longer.

Later

Have sort of forgiven Caleb for grabbing my arm and being menacing. After all, he is only looking out for Lily. He is still eligible for payback, though. No one menaces me without consequences!

Later

Have questioned Lily about her dark sensibilities. In response, she has shown me her extensive collection of interesting dead insects (found, not killed), which she has accumulated over the years while working in the family garden. Pretty impressive!

Have also questioned Lily about the unusual plants in said garden. Turns out she used to water the plot with dark elixir. Excellent!!!!!!

ME: You like plants a lot?

LILY: Oh, yes! Opal and Mother and I love to watch green things grow.

ME: It's a kickass garden, Lily. In my time we'd say you have a green thumb.

L: And do you have a green thumb too?

Lily's bug collection!

ME: Nah, it's more of a black thumb.

L: You kill plants?

ME: Oh flamjacks no. The black ones just grow really well for me.

Later

Have grilled Lily for everything she knows about the dark elixir/black rock fountain in her basement. Here is what I have learned:

1. Even when Lily was still a baby, Pearl would take her down to the basement to play in the dark fountain.

2. And would tell her stories of the Dark Girls who lived centuries ago, like Great-Aunt Aimée, back in the 900s, who used HER dark elixir to influence people's dreams.

3. She doesn't know for certain where the stuff comes from.

4. But back when Lily was 6, Aunt Millie paid Pearl a visit, and Lily overheard them saying something that made her think dark elixir came from dead Dark Girls. [CUE CHILL DOWN MY SPINE!!!]

5. But these days, she thinks she must have misunderstood. Anyway, there aren't any Dark Girls buried in her basement.[30]

---

30 That she knows of!!!!!!

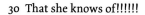

① RARE! 2 Headed Gypsy Mantis   ③ Earwig Deadicus   ⑤ El Dragoon Spy   ⑦ Angoumois Skull Moth
② Old Man Praying Weevil   ④ Gator Nayfly   ⑥ Reversible Fang Moth   ⑧ Broken Hearted Narcissiptus

6. Pearl always said that when she was old enough, Lily would discover a special talent using the dark elixir.
7. That happened when she was 11. Opal fell seriously ill. Doctors said there was nothing they could do. Lily poured dark elixir over her sister's body, and she instantly recovered.
8. She has been healing family friends and neighborhood animals ever since then.
9. But she was surprised when I told her all the different uses I'd found for the liquid black rock I'd brought back from Great-Aunt Emma's place.
10. She has never used her own elixir for anything but healing, watering the garden, and making an occasional touch-up on black clothing.
11. Though Boris suspects someone intentionally stopped the dark elixir fountain, Lily says it never even occurred to her to try controlling it.
12. So she has no explanation for why the fountain dried up and thwarted his schemes.
13. And she's more than a little worried about what Boris will do when he gets tired of waiting for the fountain to start up again.

Later

There is a dumbwaiter in this house! Nobody told me there was a dumbwaiter! Apparently nobody considers a dumbwaiter to be an alternate means of transportation. I am about to show them otherwise.

Later

I folded myself into the tiniest ball possible inside the dumb-waiter and Opal lowered me to the bottom of the shaft, which opens onto the basement. YES! The basement. I had to sit there, folded into the tiniest ball possible, for approximately forever, slowly slowly sliding open the door of the dumb-waiter and keeping a sharp watch out for henchmen, but eventually I determined that the coast was clear, and could roll myself out and breathe again.

Oh the basement, the glorious basement! The treasures! The heirlooms! The non-fountaining fountain of black rock!

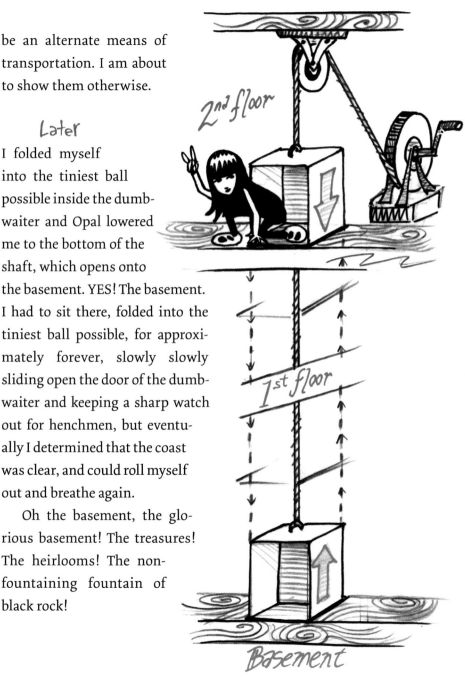

Later

Have gotten better acquainted with above-mentioned hole than I expected to. Had just pasted in the above photo when I heard the basement door opening, and boots thumping down the stairs, and henchmen voices caroling in their sweet dulcet tones. Ha. Ha. Ha. So I dived into the hole, of course. Smart move, Self. No point in hiding behind a huge, sturdy, safe, unmovable piece of furniture when there is a dirty, pitch-black, unexplored hole to dive into. Especially when said henchmen are equipped with pickaxes and shovels, and are hex-bent on expanding said hole to China.

So yeah. Imagine my horror when I realized I had chosen the worst possible hiding place in the whole basement, essentially trapping myself. It was too late to climb out—they'd see me in a second—so I looked around the hole in a panic. I don't really know what I expected to find,[31] but here's what I saw: Though at first glance the walls of the pit were the same all around, roughly hacked into the earth under the house, on SECOND glance I was sure I saw something different on one side. I know it sounds bizarre, but it was like a light was shining through the dirt at that place. Only . . . it wasn't light EXACTLY . . . it was darkness.

Yes. I saw darkness shining through the dirt. OK? That's my story, and I'm sticking to it.

Anyway, I started digging with my hands at that spot, and found the dirt falling away easily, quickly revealing an open space beyond the pit. I dove through that hole right before the henchmen started throwing their tools into the pit. Then I hurried to block up my tunnel again before they saw it. Luckily there were enough rocks at hand to do the job—as good a job as I could do for the moment, anyway. Am now sitting here by the spot, listening to the men on the other side, and writing by the tiny light of my spy-cam, since it is pitch-dark in here. Heard the thugs lower themselves into the pit and commence their digging, complaining loudly all the while. They don't seem to have noticed my little doorway. Fingers crossed they never will!

OK—more later. I have exploring to do.

---

31 Was half expecting to find some dead Dark Girls, if you want to know the dead dark truth.

Later

Excellent! What I've busted through to is some kind of underground passageway. Not really sure what it is for, and am navigating mostly by touch. It seems sturdy, dry, and well built. Will definitely explore it thoroughly when I have the time. And possibly a lantern. For now, am just moving blindly forward, marking my path with paper clips in case I need to find my way back.

Later

Have found[32] a ladder leading up to some kind of trapdoor. Am going to investigate.

Later

Am outside!!! Am very dusty!!!!! People are staring!!!!!!!!! More later.

Later

I never thought I'd say this, but I wish I had the 1790s outfit on. I have scandalized the town with my indecent display of Armes and Legges. Before I finally found a convenient abandoned warehouse to duck into, I actually saw parents putting their hands over their children's eyes to save them from the spectacle of the

---

32 "Found" = "bumped into, face-first."

depraved immorality that is ME.

Good stuff!—But not so ideal for staying undercover.

Later

For a smallish 1790s seaside town, Seasidetown is marvelously well supplied with warehouses, particularly warehouses that don't seem to be guarded. This one I've chosen to hide in is WONDROUS! Tons of delightfully mysterious unopened crates, or should I say, crates that were unopened before I came on the scene.

Here are a few of the fabulous, extraordinary treasures I've found:

1. Foodstuffs—kind of stale, but the hominy looks all right, and the potatoes are only a little sprouty.
2. Enough embroidery needles and thread to supply an entire modern city full of ironically crafting hipsters.
3. Assorted 1790s metal machine parts. Oh flamjams of ecstasy!
4. Assorted 1790s patent "medicines," featuring ingredients like arsenic and mercury.

NOTE TO SELF:
Do not get sick in the 1790s.

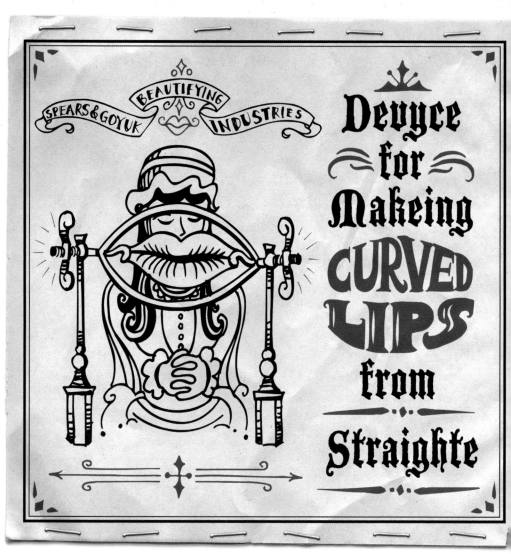

5. Assorted 1790s misguided inventions.
6. Assorted 1790s toys. Am amazed what kids of this
   day were making do with. I mean, are whistles even
   considered toys anymore?

7. Pamphlets on why women should be allowed to vote.
8. Pamphlets on why slavery should be abolished.
9. Pamphlets on why slavery should NOT be abolished. Oh boy.
10. Rats, and several tons of their droppings.
11. Tea, tea, tea, tea, tea.
12. Extremely horrible-looking medical apparatus, e.g., tools used to make the ill person bleed. Just what you need when you're feeling poorly—heavy bleeding.
13. A bale of Young Ladies' Apparel. Terrible styles, but they will save me from public outrage, arrest, and/or stoning.

Later

Am out and about in the town. I love this place. As long as I don't have to live here permanently, that is. It is no quiet, quaint seaside village, but a nasty, bustling, urban city, full of Europeans, West Indians, Africans, miscellaneous sailors, ladies of loose morals, you name it. Lots of languages, lots of smells, lots of exciting new (old) swearwords. Have been loitering around the wharves, where most of the action is going on.

Later

Have just finished episode of said action. It was very thrilling! I was slinking along the wharves, trying to both A) take it all in and B) somehow avoid looking like a tourist, when I spotted a large gang of young hooligans staring at me. One of them, the tallest and most likely the leader, had the nerve to call me a scurvy wench. I pulled out my slingshot and pegged him between the eyes. The entire gang then whipped out their own slingshots and let fly with rocks. I did my best to hold them off, but one of the little ruffians ran around and tried to grab me from behind. Hammerfist time![33] Once I'd put that jerk in his place,[34] I took

Ruffians on the run!

ESPrints

33 Philosophy of nonviolence kinda fell by the wayside today. Will try to do better tomorrow. Assuming no one attacks me.
34 His place being in the dirt, groaning with pain.

shelter behind a moving carriage and shot at the gang from between the horses' legs. Much howling ensued. No horse was harmed. Left the lads squirming in the dust and made tracks.

Later—evening

Have located Boris' medicine show caravan in the town square. Imagine my surprise when I found out he is apparently still selling his Fever Reliever!!!!! Must get my hands on a bottle as soon as possible!!!! Unfortunately, the caravan is closed for the night and heavily guarded. Have snooped around all I dare. Found nothing. May have to come back in the daytime and just buy a bottle.

Later

Back in the tunnel, by my secret doorway into Lily's basement. Everything seems quiet above, for now at least. Am going to make a break for the dumbwaiter in a moment. Am feeling the urgent need to get upstairs and get the rest of my relations vaccinated.

Medicine Show with Dogbeast.

Have witnessed some things that make me less enthusiastic about the 1790s in general. I had spotted a man who looked like a doctor and started following him, curious to see what this white fever epidemic was all about. Spied in the windows of the houses he went into, and the scenes I saw were not good. I've got a pretty strong stomach, but there was an awful lot of eXtreme medical gore going on in people's sickrooms. Prognosis not too good for a lot of these patients. Am concerned about Pearl and Opal and Caleb.

Later

Back upstairs. Have discussed the white fever a bit with Pearl. Apparently no one in the 1790s realizes it is spread by mosquitoes. They believe it comes from contaminated air. So, unfortunately, here we are in midsummer, and everyone has their windows open, airing their homes and letting in the deadly bloodsuckers. Also, the window screen has not been invented. Nor bug spray. Nor THE WHITE FEVER VACCINE. Sigh!!!! Luckily for Lily's family, Boris has nailed shut all their windows, so at least they don't have a mosquito problem.[35] Am going to try to talk them into getting their shots anyway, just to be safe.

---

35 Just a hot/stuffy/chamber-pot-scented-air problem.

Later

Late. Cannot sleep. Am writing by the tiny light of my spy-cam so as not to wake up Lily.

Have been thinking a lot about this dry, dark fountain in Lily's basement, and how much Boris and I both want it to start up again. Hate to admit it, but Boris and I have something else in common: We both believe someone (in my case, Lily) has the power to control that fountain. It started flowing the day she was born, and stopped two days after Boris started stealing the elixir. What are the odds?

It's not that I think Lily's lying to us. It's obvious that she doesn't have the spine to stand up to Boris after even one day of hunger. I think she just doesn't know her own abilities yet.

Reeeeeeeeeeeeally hope this is not wishful thinking on my part . . . but I think I might be able to help.

Monday, August 9, 1790

Today's assignments:
- Get relatives vaccinated—13 points
- Cope with painfully diurnal sleep schedule—113 points
- Get hands on Fever Reliever (LATE!!)—131,313 points
- Begin homeschooling Lily in a 1790s version of Jedi training—1313 points

Caleb was just here on fresh water/chamber pot/smushed bread duty. He helped me talk Pearl and Opal into letting me vaccinate them. I really don't think they would have agreed if he hadn't insisted. They were nervously pooh-poohing my arguments and insisting they were safe, and I was just about to launch into a description of what I'd seen in the sickrooms—the white, ashy skin; the toxic, useless medicines; the chalky sweats; the milky vomit—but Caleb saw it in my mind and saved me the trouble.

CALEB: Mrs. Étrange, Miss Opal, this is a medical necessity. In fact [rolling up his sleeve], I shall be the first to receive the medicine.

ME: Righty right. [Cleaning the needle and Caleb's arm with cyder.] [Cyder: the beverage best enjoyed untasted.] I'll just count to three. One . . . [Jabbing him before I got to two.]

C: Blast!!

PEARL: Heavens!

C: Begging your pardon, madam!

ME: Who's next?

Later

Am SLEEPY. It was not easy getting up at daybreak o'clock with Lily, Opal, and Pearl today. Have quizzed Lily on whether she wouldn't prefer to sleep all day and stay up all night, like I usually do. She stared at me with her mouth open until I told her something was bound to fly into it. When she finally collected her wits, here's what she had to say on the topic:

LILY: You mean, you actually sleep in the DAYTIME?

ME: Yep. And I'm up all night. Nocturnal. Like the cats and bats and rats.

L: But . . . I don't understand. Your mother allows this?

ME: Yeah. She's used to it. I'm just that way.

L: [Dreamily.] Once, on a Saturday, Mother forgot to wake me, and I slept until noon. It was wonderful.

ME: [Rolling my eyes.] Really? Noon, huh? How nice of her.

L: As it turned out, she was dreadfully ill in bed, and Opal was tending her, and no one thought of me all morning.

ME: Gotcha. And did you feel like a terrible, slovenly slugabed?

L: A bit.

ME: But I bet you would really enjoy being nocturnal. Am I right?

L: In truth . . . I would LOVE it.

ME: Hey, I think you might need to explain to your mom that as one of the Dark Girls, you are naturally nocturnal, and that you need your nighttime fun, and that's just the way it has to be.

L: Oh, I don't think I could do that. She would be so horribly disappointed in me if I were ever to disagree with her.

ME: Lily, Lily, Lily, Lily, Lily. Your mom's a really nice person, a lot like my own mom. In fact, I don't think your mom is the problem at all. I think the problem is you.

L: [Sniffling. Getting vapory.] But . . . I can't . . . It's not my . . . I'm just a girl!

ME: B*GR!TT!NG H^FFE*R%TS!!!!!! Lily Étrange, you are a DARK GIRL. Don't you see how PHENOMENAL that is? Now listen here, missy, I have HAD IT with your whiffling and vaporing. Do you realize this town is full of dying people? And that you have the power to heal them? Isn't that kind of amazing? . . . Now go sit in the corner and think about what I said.

L: [Blinking at my outburst. Taking it all in.] No. I'm not sitting in the corner. This is MY room.

ME: Hey, yeah! Now we're getting somewhere!

L: I used to love healing people, Cousin Emily. And

	Uncle Boris took that away from me. He makes me feel so helpless! Sometimes, when I think about him, I get a little . . . well . . .
ME:	Enraged? Incensed? Infuriated?
L:	Well, those words sound very unladylike. I'm . . . concerned. Troubled. Uneasy, Cousin Emily. And I . . . I think I'm ready to do something about it.
ME:	That's the spirit. I guess.
L:	We need to summon my dark elixir, don't we?
ME:	Not "we," Lily. YOU.

Later

It has begun. I've drawn on a lifetime of knowledge taken from sitting in on my mom's yoga classes, reading biographies of Helen Keller, and watching old kung fu movies, and have constructed a program of intense mental and physical discipline for young Lily. She may or may not learn to summon her dark elixir, but flagdrak it, she WILL come out of this with a can-do attitude and improved upper body strength, or I'll eat Enigma's severed tail, with gritts on top!

Later

Lily is a difficult case, man. I thought we could start by toughening her up a bit physically, maybe build her endurance, but she does not have the basic confidence necessary to do a single jumping jack.[36] Forget shadow boxing, or meditation in the vulture pose. We had to break for tea and go over some basic theory of girl power first. To her credit, she is very willing to learn, and it's hardly her fault that she sees herself (and all other females) as helpless, mindless, and muscle free. She has never known anything else. It was kind of thrilling to see her expression as I told her some inspirational tales of ladies like Suzy "Bug" Ramirez, inventor of the structural assay parser;[37] Dottie Winston, discoverer of the elusive aquatic cats of Venice, Italy; and Venus Fang Fang, legendary trainer of secret agents and creator of the spy diaper. Another couple of lessons like this, and she may be ready to do her first push-up.

Later

Did not realize that being a motivational trainer would be so rough on the old patience. Also, I am clearly not cut out for the job. It goes against all I believe to encourage anyone to do ANYTHING to improve themselves. But Lily's a relative, and so obviously in need of some gentle kicking in the derriere. And, OK, I should be completely honest with myself here and admit that helping Lily also has the potential to help ME, if it improves her chances of getting her dark elixir flowing again. Still, I desperately need some quality alone time. Left Lily still

---

36 Nor the wardrobe for it.

37 As well as the less renowned (but insanely useful) test-tube cozy.

practicing that push-up and snuck out via dumbwaiter into the underground passageway. Have brought a candle this time. Am ready to explore.

Later

There are doors down here! Yes, doors!!! All locked, but all unlockable (with the right tools—thank badness for paper clips, hairpins, and wire). Most of the doors lead to more passageways, but one opened onto a small rough-cut room containing an extremely old-looking table and chairs, and nothing else. FASCINATING!!!! Will bring Lily here as soon as I feel she deserves it.

Later

Have looked closely at the ground in all the tunnels, but haven't seen any footprints except my own. There is a thick layer of dry,

dusty dirt that would probably show tracks pretty well. Am happy to say I don't think anyone has been down here in years.

Later

My candle is burning out, so will have to abandon exploring for a while. Am about to head up that ladder into town. Am planning to visit Boris' caravan and try to buy a bottle of Fever Reliever. FINGERS CROSSED!

Later

Plans have not been going well! First off, I really should have given more thought and preparation to my first meeting with Uncle Boris. Specifically, I should have considered my resemblance to Lily, and the fact that I'm wearing her clothing, and how he might react.

Here's how he reacted:

BORIS: LILY? Oh . . . my mistake, young lady. You look much like a young relative of mine.

ME: [Super uncomfortable.] Ha ha ha ha ha ha! How amusing. May I have a bottle of black rock, please?

B: What's that, now? Black ROCK?

ME: [Even MORE uncomfortable.] Sorry, I meant dark elixir.

B: [Looking HIGHLY suspicious.] Dark elixir? Now where did you hear that phrase, I wonder? Perhaps you do know my niece Lily after all?

ME: Nooooooooo, I'm sure I don't. Never heard the name before in my life.

B: [Suddenly all charm.] Are you alone, young lady? Where are your parents?

ME: [Gulping.] Sick in bed, sir. They sent me out to buy your Fever Reliever. Everyone knows it's the only cure for the dread white fever.

B: [Distracted by flattery, as I'd hoped.] Yes, indeed it's a miracle, a very miracle of medicinal majesty! Step right up, folks, pay your jack and take home your cure. Black Potion for White Fever!

ME: How much jack, sir?

B: Quarter jack a bottle, my dear girl. But what price can be placed on life?

I nodded and did my best to melt away into the crowd. Returned to Lily's house, wondering how much I expected a quarter jack to be worth, and how likely Lily was to let me borrow it from her. Would like to know how many people are paying it. And, more to the point: Is it really dark elixir in those bottles?

Later—back in the house with Lily

Lily has confirmed what I suspected: She does not have a quarter jack. In fact, she said that Pearl would have to raid their life savings to get anything close to that amount. I assured her there was no need, and we would just have to get our hands on a bottle of dark elixir some other way.

Later

Lily has managed to do two complete push-ups. I took that as a victory and tried to move on to sit-ups. That's when I discovered she wears a corset, which is a demented sort of torture implement that prevents women from bending, breathing, or surviving childbirth. Lily pointed out that it provides excellent back support. I pointed out that she should take responsibility for supporting her own back and not ask some innocent whalebones to do it for her. She was unfamiliar with the phrase "take responsibility." Apparently no one ever tells girls of the 1790s to take responsibility for anything. Am a little jealous of them in spite of myself.

Anyway. I have insisted Lily take off the corset and not wear it again. She finally agreed, but is clearly afeared of what Pearl will say. Next lesson will have to be Mother/Daughter Relationship!

Later

Lily is having a hard time with the current lesson, and flat-out did not believe me when I told her I address my mom as Patti. I tried to explain that she can have a relationship of mutual respect with her mother, but she seems to think the world will implode if she so much as tells her mother "no." Am sorry to say that her neurosis is rubbing off on me, and I now suspect Aunt Pearl of being a violent raging dictator behind that sweet façade.

ouch!

ME: C'mon, Lily, you're living in the time of some of the greatest rebels history has known. Can't you take some inspiration from them?

LILY: I suppose you're referring to the revolutionaries? They may have rebelled against King George, but I doubt they contradicted their mothers.

Clearly, we are not making much progress, so we'll have to put this lesson aside and revisit it tomorrow. Draxty halfbacks! I really wanted to get back onto a nocturnal schedule tonight.

Later

One sit-up. Progress.

Later—way past Lily's bedtime

Focused meditation (though NOT in vulture pose). I asked Lily to lie on her bed, close her eyes, and imagine she was with a dying person. Then she was to visualize saving their life. She lay there perfectly still for twenty-three minutes, then her eyes snapped open and she jumped up and grabbed my arm.

LILY: I can't summon the dark elixir, Cousin Emily! I can't!

ME: Sure you can! I know you can do it!

L: No, you don't understand. I had a vision of myself in the basement, where my fountain used to be. And I was filled with that wonderful feeling of wanting to heal the sick with the elixir. But then I saw the fountain bubbling up again, and all I felt was terror! Because Boris will take it away from me again! I can't summon the elixir just for him to take it!

ME: [Thinking of Blackrock, coming unmoored in

space and time.] I hear you, Lily. Hey, what if we tried to summon the black rock somewhere else? I mean, wouldn't it be cool if we could make a new fountain somewhere Boris couldn't find it?

L: That would be very . . . "cool."

ME: K, I know this great warehouse . . .

Later

We are still in Lily's room. She has made some progress, but not enough to leave the house in the middle of the night without her mother's permission. Oh well. Baby steps, man.

Tuesday, August 10, 1790

Today's assignments:
- Persuade Lily to leave the house with me—13 points
- Remain patient with Lily's "I'm just a girl" attitude— 33 points
- Guide Lily toward new attitude of Dark Girl Pride— 113 points
- Get hands on Fever Reliever (LATE!!)—313,131,313 points

Pearl came knocking at the door shortly after sunrise to see what was keeping her two slugabeds. I groaned and buried my head under Mystery, but could still clearly hear the following exchange:

LILY:	Cousin Emily and I are sleeping late today.
PEARL:	[Sharp intake of breath.] Lily! Are you poorly?
L:	No, Mother, we're just tired, and we're sleeping late today.
P:	Why, Lily, I never . . .
L:	Please close the door on your way out.

Later—Noon-thirty

Could have slept another four hours, myself, but am very proud of Lily, who has said no to her mother AND slept past noon for the first time in her life. I admit I was nervous for her when we finally went into Pearl's room for lunch, but Pearl was her usual sweet self and said nothing about her daughter's outrageous rebellion.

Finally, Lily finished her hominy, put down her spoon, took a deep breath, and announced her plan to start sleeping all day and staying up all night.

Pearl immediately started to cry.

LILY:	Oh, Mother! I am so sorry! I didn't mean—
P:	Oh, it's just like Aunt Millie said it would be. You're becoming a young lady! Ohooohhoooohhhhhh! [Sobbing into her handkerchief.]
OPAL:	Motherrrrrrrrrr?
L:	What on earth do you mean?
P:	Oh, Aunt Millie told me that this would

116

happen to you. I'm just so proud of you, my dear. Ohhoooohhhhhooooohooo!

ME: [Silently sneaking away from this emotional family scene.]

Whew! Did not expect THAT reaction. Hope Lily is up to the strain of it all.

NOTE TO SELF:
Should question Pearl on what else Aunt Millie told her about raising a Dark Girl!

Later

Was able to catch a delicious catnap (with two cats piled on me) while Lily and her mother had their little heart-to-heart. Finally Lily returned to her bedroom, a strange new look in her eyes. It looks a little like . . . confidence, I think.

ME: So Lily. How'd all that go?

LILY: Oh, very well, thank you.

Mother always knew I would eventually go nocturnal.

ME: Great, so, not much of a beating, then?

L: Tee hee! Only a very mild beating today!

ME: Ahhahhahhaahhah!!!! Lily, my friend, I think you just made your first joke. And seriously, good work. I was getting really sick of this up-at-sunrise routine.

L: Yes, well, I still feel like a slovenly slugabed, so let's get back to the lessons.

Later

Lily and I spent most of the afternoon discussing girl power, brainstorming ways of summoning the dark elixir, and working on that difficult third push-up. Also, had our first lesson in Introductory Slingshottery. Lily has a long row to hoe when it comes to slingshot mastery. Half the time she ends up hitting herself in the head with the slingshot or the projectile. Luckily we are using balls of paper instead of rocks, or she'd have a concussion by now.

POP QUIZ

1. True or False? The use of rocks, knives, and
   lead balls as ammunition by neophyte projectile
   weapon users is a commendable practice.

2. There comes a time in every Dark Girl's life
   when she and her mother must discuss:
   a) Growing Up
   b) Becoming a Young Lady
   c) Leading a Nocturnal Lifestyle

Later

Was having a grand old time laughing my cheeks off at Lily's comic efforts with yon slingshot, but eventually noticed that the afternoon was wearing into evening, and decided the time was ripe for a second visit to Uncle Boris' caravan. Am in the tunnel now. About to head outside. Will write more later.

Later

Ugh! Tunnel not so dry today. Must have been those early-morning rains. Am very mucky. Seems to be less muddy further on, at least. Am glad Lily's clothing is already black.

SUCCESS!!!!!!!! Have managed to swipe a bottle of Fever Reliever using a clever diversion to distract the guards from the merchandise. After standing around outside the medicine show for nearly an hour trying to figure out a plan, I suddenly spotted that gang of junior roughnecks ambling down the street. Promptly recalled Caleb's lie about street youths attacking the medicine show. Well, when inspiration hollers, Emily listens! I whipped out my slingshot and let fly at the leader and his upper echelon of child thugs. They came roaring across the street at me, but I led them into the crowd and disappeared around the other side of the caravan. Townspeople immediately started to whack the ruffians about the head and shoulders with their newspapers, satchels, bindlestaffs, what-have-you, and with just a few more well-aimed missiles from my slingshot, I was able to cultivate a small-scale riot. AHHAHHAHAAAHAH! I LOVE small-scale riots!!! I crawled under the main wagon and waited for the guard to leave his post, then gaffled a bottle of medicine and bailed as fast as possible. Am headed back to Lily's for some testing.

FAILURE!!!!!!!! Should have known Boris couldn't still be selling the real stuff. Sad to say, whatever's in this bottle won't make my Time-Out Machine work, and it won't heal this blister I've got on my toe, and Lily has pointed out that it smells like moleasses. HUGE disappointment! No time to dwell on that now, though. I have to get right back out there and forage for our dinner.

Later

Evening at last. Have just come back from disheartening food run. The market I'd been to on Sunday was closed, with a sign on the door:

Could not find any other markets, so I had to settle for some sprouty potatoes from my favorite warehouse. Y'know, now that I'm thinking about it, Seasidetown is looking a lot less bustling than it did two days ago. Epidemic is taking its toll, apparently.

Later—finally dark

We have just finished eating a dinner of sprouty potatoes and the rest of the hominy. Am getting tired of 1790s food. Am having tantalizing visions of big, squashy avocado sandwiches full of horseradish and black pepper. Must get back to my own time soon. Must get T.O.M. running. Must encourage Lily to summon dark elixir!

Later

Am encouraging Lily to summon for all she is worth. This consists mainly of her lying on her bed, meditating on all the sick people in town and how much they could use her healing abilities. Am still mixing this up with cardiovascular exercises, strength training, and the occasional martial arts technique, just for the confidence it seems to give her. But overall, I think the way to inspire Lily's successful summoning is through her tender little heart.[38]

No dark elixir yet, but Lily is clearly benefiting from the effort, based on her improved posture and that happy gleam in her eye. That can't be hurting our chances, right?

Later

Hunger has given my arguments a little more urgency, I guess,

---

38 There's a gory joke in there somewhere . . .

because I have finally talked Lily into leaving the house tonight. I painted a very enticing picture of "my" warehouse: its privacy, its security, its foodstuffs . . . Eventually Lily broke down and agreed to accompany me. Not without some terror, mind you. Am excited for her to get out and about and enjoy the night for once. OK—gotta go get my 1790s gear on. More later.

Later

I am incredibly proud of Lily for A) folding herself into the tiniest ball possible and getting into the dumbwaiter; B) sneaking past sleeping henchmen and into the pitch-black hole in the basement floor; C) traveling through mucky tunnels, up a creaky ladder, and out a cobwebby trapdoor; and D) slinking around town with me in the middle of the night, when no respectable young lady would DREAM of being outdoors. We are now hanging out, UNCHAPERONED, in the warehouse, poking around in the crates and having a good old time. We will probably need to settle down and get to summoning in a bit, but I want Lily to get a taste of her freedom, so she will know that it's . . . well, tasty.

Lily is much more fun without her corset, her mother, and her inhibitions!!!

Later

Had hoped that Lily would try to do some summoning in the warehouse. Had thought she might feel less constrained here, less threatened by Boris and thugs. Would like nothing better than a big old geyser of molten black rock to burst through the floor and sweep us off our feet, screaming and laughing with joy. I WISH! Instead, she is absorbed with poking through the crates and loading up a basket with foodstuffs. Have decided to leave her alone and let her summon where and when she wants to. This is her summoning, not mine!

Later

Back at home. Almost dawn. Lily and I are pooped. No black rock yet. Hope we have better luck tomorrow.

Wednesday, August 11, 1790

Today's assignments:
- Encourage summoning—13 points
- Catch up on sleep—13 points
- Explore opportunities for extended learning and discussion on Dark Girls—163 points

Lily and I were allowed to sleep all day (YESSS!) and woke up just in time for dinner. I took the opportunity to quiz Pearl a bit on A) exactly how she recognized me as a Dark Girl, and B) what Great-Aunt Millie told her about raising a Dark Girl. She told me that she knew <u>beyond a doubt</u> the moment she saw me that I was like Lily and Millie. She said it was a little in the set of my mouth, and how I move, but mostly it's in my eyes, and their special kind of . . . dark quality, I guess. And thinking back to the first time I saw Lily, I kind of know what she means. I didn't question it at the time, but I knew for sure that the girl in front of me was one of my Dark Aunts. And now I guess I know why.

Pearl also told me that Millie gave her the following guidelines:

1. Mothers of Dark Girls are advised to give their daughters free rein in all matters pertaining to their dark elixir.
2. Ditto for nocturnal habits.
3. The wearing of black clothing is to be expected and allowed.
4. Any feline companions are to be respected and cared for like members of the family.
5. Attendance in regular school can be encouraged to the degree that the Dark Girl accepts it.
6. Ditto for various social activities (organized religion, organized sports, organized socializing . . .).
7. However, SOME kind of education is to be pursued.
8. And strict instruction in family history, with special emphasis on the lives of other Dark Girls, is MANDATORY.
9. Collections of unusual objects are to be tolerated. In fact, outbuildings may need to be rented.
10. The occasional trance, reverie, daze, sleepwalking spell, or episode of speaking in tongues is to be humored

without summoning a doctor.

11. The occasional unexplained (or poorly explained) absence from home is to be tolerated without alerting the authorities.

12. Once The Talent emerges, it is to be cultivated, no matter how odd.

13. Any negative attitudes toward things supernatural had best just be thrown out the window. In short, be prepared for the weird stuff!

Welly welly welly welly welly welly well!!!!!!

CLEARLY, my mother has some explaining to do.[39]

Because CLEARLY, she knows perfectly well what I am.[40]

Later

There was quite a surprise waiting for me and Lily when we returned to "our" warehouse this evening for summoning practice: a family of five, huddled among the boxes, and just as surprised to see us as we were to see them.

They are John Ebenezer; his wife, Hannah; son James (age eleven); other son Matthew (age nine); and daughter, Deborah, called Sweetie-Pie (age three). Their home caught fire today and

---

39 "Aunts alive today? Sorry, E, I don't know of any." Harrumph!!!!

40 See items #2, 3, 4, 5, 6, 7, 8, 9, 10, 11, and 13 above.
Cheeeeeeeeeze!!!!

The Ebenezer family.

the fire brigade never came. Mr. Ebenezer says most of the members of the fire brigade are sick, dead, or at their summer homes, waiting out the white fever. Same goes for the police. The doctors are dropping of exhaustion, and storekeepers (as I well know) have closed up shop.

ME: Can't they bring in help from other towns?
MR. EBENEZER: Who would come here? Everyone fears the
               white fever.

Am now kind of wishing I brought more vaccine. Having met Mr. Ebenezer and his family, I feel pretty uncomfortable knowing their chances of survival depend on whether or not they've had any mosquito bites in the past week.

ME:	Hey, have any of you had any mosquito bites in the past week?
THE EBENEZERS:	[Looking at me as if I am insane.] Certainly. Perhaps. Not me. I don't know. 'Squito?
ME:	Well, don't get any more, OK? Cover yourselves up, stay inside, whatever it takes.
HANNAH:	What in heaven for, Miss Emily?
ME:	Oh, well, your doctors don't understand this yet, but it's the mosquitoes that spread the white fever.
LILY, JOHN, HANNAH, JAMES, AND MATTHEW:	[Laughing heartily at me.]
ME:	No, seriously . . . Oh, never mind. Just do me a favor and avoid the suckers.

Later

After questioning the Ebenezers, I think it is safe to say that no one else has visited this warehouse since I discovered it. They were pretty sure it was abandoned when they chose it as their shelter for the night. Am starting to wonder if perhaps the owner is lying in his house somewhere, drinking toxic medicines, and wasting toward death. Or has he gathered up his belongings and family members and skipped town completely? Then again, maybe he just took a few days off and will be back in action tomorrow. The town is noticeably quieter than it was even yesterday. There's kind of an ominous, silent feeling everywhere. Of course, with the white fever epidemic killing dozens of people every day, there's not much of a party atmosphere. People are probably just staying quietly indoors, hoping to ride it out.

Later

While the cats are busy patrolling the warehouse, and Lily is off enjoying her first three human friends,[41] I have been doing my best to get a history lesson out of John and Hannah Ebenezer. They are both children of former slaves (!!!!!!!!!!) who fled to Seasidetown years ago. Have not yet managed to get the topic of conversation around to the fact that I'm From The Future, but when/if I do, I look forward to letting them know that slavery will indeed (eventually) be abolished, and that their children's children's children's children have a decent shot at equality. Oh, wait. Make that grandchildren's grandchildren's grandchildren's grandchildren. Oh, wait. Actually, considering my general low opinion of Humanity, I had better stay off the topic entirely, or I will crush their courageous, optimistic spirits.

---

41 I don't entirely approve of this. But . . . I guess I don't entirely disapprove, either. I almost applauded when they started using miscellaneous 1790s contraptions as musical instruments.

Later

I eventually realized that the Ebenezers are not nocturnal like us, and have had a long, sad, and exhausting day. Have had to break up Lily's Social Hour so that we could say our goodbyes. The conversation was going a little bit like this:

MICHAEL: When I grow up, I'm going to be the chief of police!

JAMES: Oh? When I grow up, I'm going to be the head of the fire brigade!

SWEETIE-PIE: When I grow up, I'ma be the mayor!

LILY: [Looking shy.] When I grow up, I'm going to be that weird old lady that all the kids are scared of!

ME: [Interrupting.] If I grow up, I'm gonna be the Evil Overlord of the Universe, and if you're nice, maybe I'll let you visit me in my Magical Floating Palace in the Sky.

L/J/M/SP: [Hushed silence as everyone contemplates such intriguing accommodations.]

Later

Lily and I are in the tunnels again. It's still mucky down here, even muckier than before, though mostly just outside my little doorway from the basement. Must be a leak around here. Oh well.

Enigma and Mystery have been having themselves a fine frisk-about in spite of the mud, and Lily and I are thoroughly enjoying The Exploration Effort. We've been trying to figure out what the heck these passageways were built for. (No sign of dead Dark Girls—more's the pity!) As well as who built them, and when. So far, no clue. I mean, based on the dust and cobwebs, it seems like no one's been down here in decades, yet it's not like the tunnels are crumbling either. They're definitely not for sewage. Seasidetown is still decades away from any concept of plumbing.[42]

Later

Have shown Lily the Boardroom—briefly. She'd barely stepped a foot inside before she turned and hustled right back out.

ME: You OK, Lily?

LILY: [Voice made shaky by her shuddering.] Uncanny . . . place . . . !

ME: C'mon, Lily. Look at me . . . look at YOU! WE'RE uncanny. Let's go back in and check it out, huh?

L: [Clearing her throat. Straightening her shoulders—with effort.] Maybe . . . later.

---

42 That, and I kind of prefer to believe they are the work of giant mutant mole monsters. Am keeping that theory to myself.

Later

Have found something very intriguing—a series of letters carved into a post!

ME: I think it's a code! M.E. wanted M.K. to come see them in the A.M. Don't you think?

LILY: Perhaps . . . but . . .

ME: Yeah, I really have nowhere else to go with that thought.

L: [Kindly.] Let's keep exploring, shall we?

A lot later

Excellent night!!!! We have been in the tunnels for hours, and I think we've mapped them all. Here's the incredible part: The map seems to form some kind of symbolic shape. Check it out:

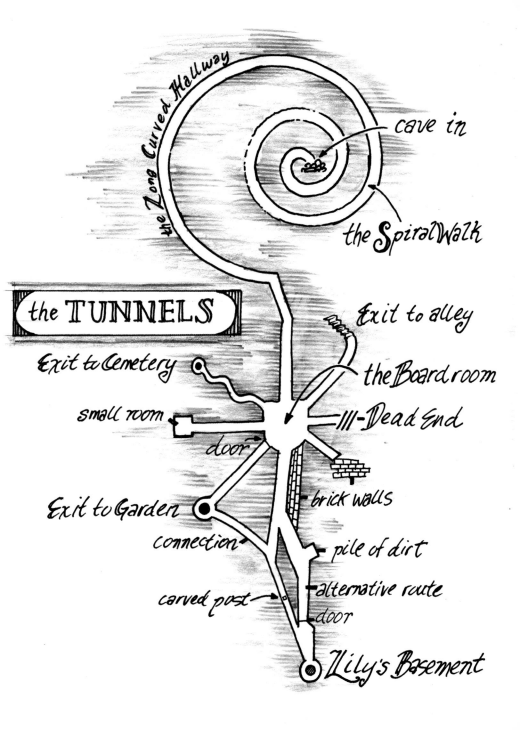

Neither Lily nor I recognize this symbol. Wait, that's not exactly what I mean. I mean that we've never seen it before. As soon as we'd been through the last unexplored tunnel, and I drew in the final remaining piece of the map, we both looked at the completed shape, and . . . we KNEW it.

This is one of THOSE places.

Like the secret closet under Aunt Emma's house in Blackrock. A place Dark Aunts have flourished. I could feel it the first time I jumped into the pit in Lily's basement—the way my eyes sharpened up and showed me the way into the tunnels.

I told Lily this, and all she did was nod and say, "Let's go back to the Boardroom."

Later

PROGRESS!!!!! And even more mystery. We'd been hanging out

in the Boardroom for a while, speculating on who made it and what it was used for. Lily was still calling it "uncanny," but no longer running away. She's right, though, y'know—I could feel that whatever unusual quality is in the tunnels was strongest right there in that room.

I was just idly roaming around, thinking the above thought, running my hands over the table, when something caught my eye: another set of letters carved faintly into the back of one of the chairs.

ME: Lily! Check this out, I found "EM" carved into this chair!
LILY: Are there any on the other chairs?

We ran around the room checking them all. Three of the chairs had no letters we could see, but the others had the following carved into them: NL, LC, AV, MA, MF, EM, MK, CU, AM, ME.

Let the code-breaking begin!!!!!!!!!!

Later

We've gone back to that post that had the letters on it and looked at it more closely, and sure enough, under a LOT of dust and VERY faint, we found six more sets of letters above the original four, matching the ones on the chairs.

Not that this explains ANYTHING.

All right. Lily and I are pooped and the sun will be up soon. Heading home.

Thursday, August 12, 1790

Today's assignments:
- Avoid looters—13 points
- Code-break—113 points

Opal came into Lily's room at half past sunrise this morning and woke us both up with a newsflash from her psychic boyfriend.

OPAL: Emily, Lily, please wake up. Caleb says there are looters in the streets. We must be ready for them if we're attacked.

ME: Can't Boris' henchmen handle them?

O: Most of them have fled. Here, put some clothes on and come to Mother's room.

When we joined the family, Caleb was laying out the situation for Pearl as calmly as possible, but I could tell he was worried—REALLY worried.

CALEB: Did your husband keep any sort of weaponry?

PEARL: Heavens, no!

C: Spades? Pitchforks? Scythes?

P: No, nothing like that.

C: [Eyes glazing momentarily, in a way that made me think of Jakey.] Boris is coming. Miss Emily, may I suggest you hide in the dumbwaiter?

So that's why I'm back in the tunnel, slogging through the mud. Am going to check in on the Ebenezers and make sure they are not getting looted.

POP QUIZ!

1. In times of civic distress, most citizens can be counted upon to:
   a) stay calm and behave rationally
   b) extend a helping hand to their neighbors
   c) behave like raging savages

2. Boris was headed upstairs in order to:
   a) apologize for his wicked behavior and release my relatives from captivity
   b) ensure they were well fed and safe from raging savage looters
   c) behave like a raging savage himself

Later

I found the Ebenezers hiding from looters in the warehouse. Helped them barricade the doors with crates and boards. John had just returned from his job, which currently consists of roaming the streets with a cart yelling, "Bring out your dead!" and then carting the dead to the fields where the mass burials are being held. Hannah did not want him to go at all, but the job pays in food, which is in short supply—and, after all, looters are not super interested in a man with a cart full of dead people. Can hardly believe I am witnessing such times!

Hannah has fed me some potatoes and hominy. Extremely delicious.[43]

John says we are very lucky to have found a warehouse with some food supplies. Apparently, the farmers who normally bring produce into the city in the wee hours each morning stopped coming when word of the white fever epidemic got around. Prices started going up right away, but even so, people quickly bought whatever they could grab. Soon the markets were empty, which prompted today's looting festivities. Yes. How quickly civilization becomes chaos!

ME: And it's all because of a little mosquito.

JOHN: Miss Emily, have you ever seen a person die of the white fever? I don't understand how you can believe a tiny insect could cause such a terrible ailment.

ME: [And Now, Emily Explains to 1790s Guy . . . Germ Theory!] Well, the thing is, there are even

---

43 There's nothing like hunger to make you like 1790s food all over again.

	tinier ... creatures, sort of, called viruses, that are too small to see. And they live inside the mosquitoes. And, uh, when the mosquito bites you, some of the tiny creatures get inside your blood, and make you sick. . . . . Uh, seriously.
J:	[Polite, but unconvinced.] I see.
SWEETIE-PIE:	'Squito fish eat 'squitoes.
HANNAH:	Yes, dear. Finish your potatoes.
ME:	[Interested.] What 'squito fish are those?
H:	Oh, the children raise mosquito fish and sell them to the neighborhood children. Or they used to, anyway.
ME:	Those fish you're keeping in those jars by the window? But you've been feeding them ants. No mosquitoes in this warehouse.
JAMES:	They do best on mosquitoes, though.
MATTHEW:	[Proudly.] We all saved our fish when we ran out of our house when it burned.
H:	They couldn't have saved their shoes instead?

SP: Emily's keeping the 'squitoes out.[44]

ME: Yeah, well, I gotta put the lumber where the language is.

Later

Dude! I LOVE Sweetie-Pie! That three-year-old has pointed out something that none of the town fathers or senior physicians ever would have. The mosquito fish could save this town, if we can get enough of them out there. Have talked the boys into contributing their stock of fish, and finagled permission from Hannah for them to come out with me. Here's the funny part: I could have sworn it was Sweetie-Pie, in the end, who instructed her family to do as I wanted. I'm probably wrong. I do know that she convinced me to take her with us. Totally against my better judgment—the streets of Seasidetown are no place for a three-year-old right now. Nevertheless, she's coming with us, and she

---

44 To be completely honest, I was pleased that Sweetie-Pie noticed how neatly I'd boarded up the warehouse. Later I took her on a little tour of the space and showed her all the places I'd reinforced, booby-trapped, or otherwise secured the perimeter. By the end of our rounds she was suggesting refinements.

was VERY clear on that point.

We are off to hit the cisterns!

Later

Am exhausted. Have been out for hours (DAYLIGHT hours, mind you—hours when I should have been peacefully asleep) with James and Matthew and Sweetie-Pie, releasing fish into the town's cisterns, looking up their friends, convincing their friends to come release fish with us, convincing them to go fetch THEIR friends to come join in. No one had been allowed to leave the house in days, so they didn't take much convincing. And everyone seemed to have a secret way out of the house. Nearly every home is boarded up—some obviously empty, some just as obviously with people inside. Absolutely nothing is open for business. The wharf has been cordoned off—completely quarantined. Drastic decline in foreigners on the streets.[45] Still plenty of

---

45 From, like, hundreds down to, like, zero.

Seasidetown in the grips of white fever.

looters—we stayed out of their way. Getting kidnapped and sold into slavery is not my idea of a happy ending to this story.

Later

Have been watching Sweetie-Pie quite closely. At first it was to make sure she was OK. Three years old and all. Pretty soon that turned into watching in amazement as she led our group through the town. Not to mention watching all those boys, five to eight years older, following her pretty much unquestioningly. Yeah, I shouldn't have worried. In this town, she should be looking after ME. That little girl knows all the good shortcuts through yards and alleys, under fences, across gardens. VERY impressive!

Anyway—we have managed to find six of the boys' friends so far. Two of them have no mosquito fish. Three have a few fish each. The sixth kid has been sort of a motherlode, with many dozens of fish in jars under his bed that he's been hiding from his mother. And knowledge of two more kids with epic stashes of fish. So now we're taking a hominy break before we get back to it. Still three-quarters of the town to cover!

Later

Snack break, part two. We are all pretty hungry, and we've been foraging as we go. The Ebenezers sure know their edible plants. Plus we found an apple tree and gorged a bit on sweet juicy apples. Man, apples of the 1790s are DIFFERENT from what I'm used to.

Both tarter and sweeter somehow—spicier, even. You better believe I filled up on them. Then filled my pockets. You never know when a sweet juicy apple will come in handy for bribing hungry kids.

Later

Have encountered Ye Olde Gange of Youthefull Ruffians again. The leader's eyes went wide in fear when he spotted me. He had a rock whizzing at me from his slingshot almost instantly. I managed to catch it in my hand. Returned fire—using an apple. He caught it. Gnawed it to the core in about ten seconds. Then all of them came running over, slingshots held over their heads. His gang has lost five members in two days to the white fever. No markets are open for them to steal their daily meals from. They are in sorry shape. We have enlisted them in the mosquito fish effort—BRILLIANT! They have volunteered to take on the quarantine wharf, gardens surrounded by tall fences, and other places not easily accessible to younger children (or girls outfitted in impractical 1790s gear).

Also, pointed them in the direction of some unguarded fruit trees. They were very grateful.

Later

Looting seems to have died down a bit from this morning, and instead there are children to be seen everywhere, walking the neighborhoods, sneaking behind buildings and into gardens, and plopping tiny fish into cisterns, wells, water barrels, what-have-you. I wasn't kidding when I said they were not big on public health and safety in 1790. Every cistern is a disgusting, swarming pit of mosquito larvae! And people drink this stuff! Anyway, if the fish do their work, the town should be relatively mosquito free in a week.

It's kind of a case of too little, too late, though. And there is nothing to be done for people who already have the fever. Will just have to keep encouraging Lily to get some dark elixir summoned!

Later

OK—have seen some pretty strange stuff!!

Like I said, I was keeping close tabs on Sweetie-Pie, and after a little while I noticed she didn't actually seem to be releasing any fish. She'd plop one into a rain barrel or whatever, wait a moment, then put her hand in the water and scoop up the fish again.

So I asked her about it.

ME: Hey, Sweetie-Pie. How about leaving that fish there so it can do its work?

SWEETIE-PIE: Meryl's all done. [Moving on to next barrel.]

ME: [???] Hey, James, does Sweetie-Pie have a special pet fish or something?

JAMES: 'Course. That's Meryl.

ME: Oh, Meryl.

MICHAEL: You should see some of Meryl's tricks. You never saw a mosquito fish do anything so funny!

ME: I will make a point of it. [Catching up with Sweetie-Pie.] OK, Sweetie-Pie, so you want to keep Meryl, that's cool. But we really should leave some fish behind to eat the mosquito larvae.

SP: [Patiently.] Meryl's done. She ate them all.

ME: Oh . . . kay. Here's the thing, though. The adult mosquitoes, the ones in the air, they're just going to lay more eggs in that water, so we need to leave the fish behind to eat them. I mean . . . flagjax, it would be great if we had a way of getting rid of the adult mosquitoes, but we don't.

SP: [Nodding silently, then

walking on toward the next rain barrel.]

Yeah, so, I kinda shrugged that off and decided to just follow her, and release a fish into each rain barrel as she finished with it.

So I was pretty close when I saw her fish float.

I don't mean in the water, I mean IN THE AIR.

And here's the thing—while it's floating in the air, it's eating mosquitoes.

After I recovered from the shock, and ascertained that I was indeed awake, I asked the boys about it.

JOHN: Well, we all heard you say that the fish need to be eating the adult mosquitoes. How else are they going to do it?

ME: I've said many things in my time, kid, and I'm not QUITE delusional enough to believe the laws of physics and biology will change just because I say so.[46]

J: Well, it's different for Sweetie-Pie. She heard you. She told Meryl what to do.

ME: [Mulling this over. Deciding that since Sweetie-Pie was concerned, I was going to buy it, no questions asked.] [—OK, a FEW questions.] Has she always been able to do stuff like that?

---

46 Not since a particularly embarrassing incident when I was six.

J: Only since she started talking.
       She's been telling everyone what
       to do ever since.

ME: Three-year-olds can be like that, but
       things don't usually happen just because a three-
       year-old says they should. You do understand how
       rare she is, right?

Later

Have apologized to Sweetie-Pie for questioning her methods.
Then suggested that if more fish could be instructed on the
whole floating in the air thing, they'd find quite a tasty meal
waiting for them.

   To my semi-surprise, that's exactly what occurred.[47]

47 OK, so I don't have the power of command like Sweetie-Pie . . .
   but hey, Sweetie-Pie takes suggestions from ME. Not bad!

Later

We have been to the main square, where Uncle Boris' caravan has been parked—but there is no caravan in sight! I questioned what non-looting locals I could find, and got confirmation from two people who saw Boris split town. Interesting! Will check in with Lily and family and see what they know about this. Am taking the Ebenezer kids back to the warehouse, and getting my cheeks back to Lily's house posthaste.

Later

REALLY BAD STUFF!!!! Everyone is gone except for Mystery, who was hunkered under Lily's bed, ears plastered backward in "things have gotten really uncool and heavy" mode. No note, no clues, and no food. Am horribly anxious. I need to figure out where my relatives are!!!!!!

Much later

Am sleep-deprived, hungry, and excruciatingly worried. Am trying to collect my wits and come up with some kind of plan.

Have been sneaking peeks out the attic window at the looters. I can't believe I'm saying this, but we are very lucky that Boris boarded up the house so thoroughly. The next-door neighbors are frantically loading their valuables into a carriage while the man of the family stands guard with a musket. Next door to them, the situation is not so pretty. Looters are leaving that house with armloads of stuff. I hate to think what has happened to the occupants. Am hoping they are safely away at their summer home.

Gagging bolgfix, did Boris drag my relatives out of town with him?!? If so, where on earth would they have gone? And if not . . . well, I don't even want to follow that train of thought. Possibilities seem much too grim. Am trying hard not to panic, but I can't help freaking out about what he will do to them. Also, am trying very hard not to focus on the fact that Lily is my only hope of getting some black rock to power my Time-Out Machine. Frazzling shakatax!!!!! I do not want to live out my life in this century! I wish I had even the smallest clue where they might have gone. As well as some means of transportation. Reliable source of food would not hurt.

—OK, well, not much I am going to accomplish by cringing in the attic. Must shake off this incipient freakout, and at least do what I CAN do.

Later

Have done the following:

1. Wrote Lily a note telling her I have gone to look for her. As if that is likely to be any help at all.
2. Hid said note under her bedsheets.
3. Went to the cistern in the garden to fill a canteen with water for my journey.

4. Discovered to my unpleasant surprise just what Caleb put in said cistern on Sunday.
5. Went next door to raid their cistern instead.
6. Felt extremely glad their dogbeast was no longer on the scene.
7. Raided their vegetable garden and fruit trees while I was at it.
8. Made a bindlestaff and outfitted self as authentic <u>Hobo sapiens</u>.
9. Wished REALLY hard for that map of roads out of Seasidetown that I do not possess.
10. Wished even harder that the Time-Out Machine were pocket-sized, so I would not be forced to leave it in Lily's bedroom.
11. Shook off horrible flash attack of panic, fear, and insecurity. (Barely.)
12. Installed Mystery (to her GREAT displeasure) into her new seat in my hobo-sack.
13. And departed for Points Unknown.

Friday, August 13, 1790

Today's assignments:
- Recover from uncomfortable night spent outdoors— 13 points
- Code-break (LATE!)—113 points

Am not completely sure if this is good news or bad news, but I have been turned away at all points of exit from Seasidetown that I've found so far. By soldiers with muskets. No use trying to explain to them how white fever actually spreads (and how it doesn't); I could see the terror in their faces as I approached.[48]

I can only hope that the same has happened to Boris' caravan, and that I have a chance of finding them back in Seasidetown. Am headed home, with fingers crossed!

Much Later

SUPER BAD STUFF!!!!!!!!

Opal ate my apple.

My Time-Out Machine is GONE. No!

And Enigma has been catnapped!!!!!!!!!!!!!!!

Later

OK, so I have found Opal, Lily, and Pearl, who were already home when I arrived. Have had long, semi-hysterical conversations with

---

48 Can't say THAT'S never happened to me before.

them as to how and why these catastrophes could have occurred. On my part, I am angry enough about my missing apple and T.O.M. to make Caleb wonder again about that unpleasant family rumor about a Dark Aunt killing Lily. On Lily's part, she is none too happy at having been ordered to pack her belongings and pile into Boris' caravan, only to drive around for hours and hours, finally return to this prison of a home, have her beloved cat taken from her, and then get thoroughly scolded by ME. To be fair, I should not be blaming any of these people. What it boils down to is that A) Lily is a product of her times, and believed (up until now) that a little social taboo against a man stepping inside a young girl's bedroom would stop the evil Uncle Boris from stealing my T.O.M.; B) Uncle Boris is evil, and intelligent enough to realize that catnapping is the key to getting what he wants out of Lily; and C) Opal is half starved, and my apple looked tasty.

I WANT MY T.O.M. BACK RIGHT NOW!!!

But all in all, that is the most easily solved of my problems. I laugh to think that Uncle Boris can keep my belongings away from me for any length of time. Much more serious will be my need to exact suitable revenge on him for this little stunt, but even that pales compared to the issue of HOW I WILL GET BACK TO MY OWN TIME without that razzafrazzing APPLE. Assuming Lily can eventually make the dark elixir flow, and assuming I can then power the Time-Out Machine with it, I STILL have nothing to put in it that will get me back to the time and place I left!

Am clearly in deep doo-doo, but I may as well get to work rescuing Enigma before Lily loses all hope. She has disintegrated into tearful mush, and simply lies in bed crying for her cat. Too bad her training had not progressed further before this happened.

Later

Lily eventually dragged herself out of bed for the daily ration of smushed bread and hominy in Pearl's room. The two of us were not getting along particularly well.

LILY: [Real grumpy.] Don't—why must you sit so close?

ME: [Also real grumpy.] Mmph!! I still can't believe you thought GOOD MANNERS would keep Boris out of your room! I mean—OF COURSE he's gonna go in there and snoop around!

L: It seemed so unthinkable a week ago!

ME: Why did I even come here? I shoulda let dead aunts lie.

L: No one invited you!

ME: [Working self up into fine state of grump.] You didn't even leave me a note when Boris took you away. And I KNOW you had time, if you were able to pack all those suitcases.

L: A NOTE? I left you a note!

ME: What? Where? I never saw a note!

L: [Staring at me in super-irked disbelief. Tears threatening again.] The one hanging over my BED?

ME: [Staring at her in uncomfortable confusion.] [Running down the hall to her room.]

And there it was—embroidered in the spiderwebs, clear as anything, once you actually LOOKED:

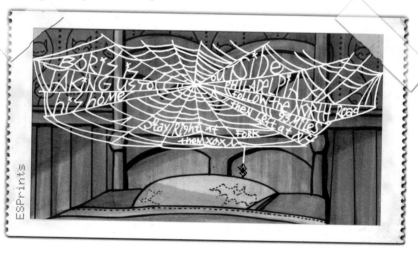

It really is a very impressive note both in content and presentation.[49] Have apologized to Lily. She has apologized to me. Tearful Mush episode thankfully over. Time to get moving.

---

49 Worth 13 out of 13 points and a shiny black star!!!

Later

Much action in the past hour! Here's what has occurred:

1. Pep-talked Lily until she was ready to be of some use to me in the rescue mission.

2. Then Lily and Mystery and I left the house via the tunnels, and soon were hunkered under Boris' caravan.

3. Sat there for several minutes before I noticed a small trapdoor in the floor of said caravan. Probably used for emptying chamber pots or something.

4. Jimmied it open with a paper clip and oh-so-cautiously poked my head up through the hole.

5. Took note of T.O.M. standing in a corner, and Boris, Musket Man, and Thugly gathered around a table, their backs to me. No sign of Enigma, though.

6. Until Thugly shifted to one side, revealing Enigma stretched out on the table, seemingly asleep.

7. Then he put down the instrument he'd been using on her. It was one I recognized from a box of horrible-looking medical apparatus I'd seen in the warehouse.

And I knew its use: bloodletting.

8. At that point, I was abruptly pushed aside by Lily, who'd been waiting her turn to get a peek inside the caravan.

9. Having gotten an eyeful of the scene described above, Lily threw to the wind the last scraps of her training, and dissolved into a (thankfully silent) puddle of vapors and snot.

10. I left her there under the caravan, with instructions to Mystery to guard her, and fled toward the wharf in search of my favorite band of underage thugs.

11. Moments later, I had made my bargain with the leader of the gang,[50] and we were all headed back to the caravan.

12. As soon as I got under it again, the slingshotting started . . . Boris and his men promptly dashed outside, as expected.

13. I popped through the trapdoor and scooped up Enigma, told Lily and Mystery to follow me, and ran for the safety of the warehouse.

Later

Left Lily and the cats at the warehouse under Hannah's care. Am back under the caravan, hoping I can get a clue as to why Boris would think it advisable to take blood from Lily's cat. I

---

50 Will be showing the whole gang how to make some wicked mods to their slingshots.

mean, I could understand holding Enigma as a hostage until he got his hands on the black potion. I could even see why he might threaten Lily with harm to her pet. But a threat's not much of a threat if you keep it private. No, this was something else, something I didn't get at all.

Boris and the henchmen returned to the caravan a few minutes after I did. I kept silent and listened. What I heard chilled me to the bone. To the MARROW. To the myelocytes INSIDE my marrow.

<table>
<tr><td>THUGLY:</td><td>Boris [he pronounced it "Boss"], the feline has escaped!</td></tr>
<tr><td>BORIS:</td><td>[Growling.] That's SIR Boris!!!—Spleeny pox-marked scut!—I told you to drain it well of blood!</td></tr>
<tr><td>T:</td><td>Indeed I drained it, Sir Boss—I heard its very heartbeats grow faint!</td></tr>
<tr><td>B:</td><td>You ratsbane! Pour the blood into this chalice—we shall see if there is anything in what Caleb says. Where IS that blasted Caleb, anyway? You—go find him. Tell him we have the witch cat's blood!</td></tr>
<tr><td>MUSKET MAN:</td><td>[Grumbling. Leaving the caravan.]</td></tr>
<tr><td>T:</td><td>He spends far too much time with the Étrange family, Sir Boss.</td></tr>
</table>

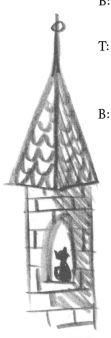

B: And that's what I pay him to do, is it not? He's wiling out that little witch's secrets for me, you shall see.

T: How difficult could it be, Sir Boss? He knows my darkest thoughts, and never hesitates to let me know. I'll wager he's hiding those secrets from you!

B: He dares not! In any case, he has already explained the difficulty. You see, my niece does not yet recognize her control over the fountain of black potion. But she is soon to understand. In fact, yesterday Caleb told me the good news that a female relation, a cousin Miss Lily's age, has come to stay with them. You wretched lazy guards—she slipped right past you! But then, she is a witch herself! It matters not—Caleb has read in her mind the good she will do Miss Lily. And already Miss Lily is making progress—coming closer every day to her full power! AHAHAHHHAHAHAH!

I felt horribly sick inside.

CALEB had suggested the catnapping.
CALEB had suggested the bloodletting.
And CALEB had told Boris about me!!!!!!!!!!!!!!!!!!!

NOTE TO SELF:
Pencil in Caleb as an ENEMY!

Inside the caravan (AKA Den of Evil.)

Later—back in the warehouse

Enigma is alive, but unconscious, and we can't wake her. Lily is getting more and more tearful, and Hannah is trying to keep her calm and do what she can for Enigma. But what is there to do? Am sitting nearby with Mystery curled in my lap. Trying to steel myself for the worst.

Later

Bad, bad news . . . and it's not about Enigma.

Lily had been sitting with Enigma in her lap, petting and talking to her. Every now and then her heartbeat would weaken, and Lily and Hannah would try their best to revive her a little, but about an hour ago I started noticing that Hannah was getting exhausted and could barely keep her eyes open. The boys

159

and I convinced her to go lie down, but just a few minutes later, Sweetie-Pie came running over to get me, so I went to look at Hannah . . . All the signs were there: the high temperature; the terrible thirst; the chalky sweat, rolling down her dark skin in grim contrast.

White fever.

Later

Have sent Michael and James out to find their father. Not that he can do anything, but he should be here with his wife, in case . . . I don't even want to finish that sentence. She has to get better, and that's ALL.

Lily, Sweetie-Pie, and I are gathered around her, encouraging her to get better, since that is the only treatment we can offer.[51]

What I wouldn't give for some dark elixir right now!

ME:	Lily? Any chance of some dark elixir?
LILY:	[Looking at me helplessly.] I wish I knew how!
SWEETIE-PIE:	What's dark elixir?
ME:	It's a . . . kind of medicine that Lily can use to heal people.
SP:	Where is it?

---

51 Luckily, Lily and Sweetie-Pie don't have the word "contagious" in their vocabularies, so I didn't have to reassure them that they couldn't get white fever from sick people.

L:	[Near tears.] I don't know!
SP:	I know! It's at your house!
L:	No, it's not—
ME:	[Excited—realization dawning.] Lily, it IS at your house! Remember the mud in the tunnel? It wasn't from the rain, Lily!
L:	Yes . . . that could be it. That could be it!

—OK, we are mobilizing—heading back to the tunnel to get some (hopefully) healing mud for Enigma and Hannah—more later—

Later

AMAZING
miraculous
mind-blowing events have transpired.

We have not left the warehouse—the dark elixir has come to us, and to the whole town.

And Lily is like a new person.

Here's what happened:

I'd been trying to get us up and out of the warehouse to fetch some dark elixir mud, but Lily didn't want to leave Enigma, and I didn't want to leave Hannah and Sweetie-Pie alone, and then Mystery gave this heartbreaking howl, and Lily looked up at me and said, "It's Enigma . . . her heart just stopped."

A terrible moment went by.

And Sweetie-Pie said, "Then make it start, Lily."

And Lily DID make it start. The lovely black rock, that is. I think all of us felt it in the marrow of our bones, a sort of psychic pull, a weird kind of suction, like the dark attraction of a black hole. And it was coming from Lily. And it was bringing the dark elixir. No little stream, but a massive torrent rushing through the tunnels, filling the underground passageways, bursting out of all the exit points, flooding the streets.

We ran outside, scooping it up in our hands, rushing it in to our sick and dying.

And all over town, people were doing the same.

POP QUIZ!

1. We can thank ___ for giving Lily control over
   the black rock.
   a) my training program
   b) her concern for Enigma
   c) Sweetie-Pie's voice of command
   d) all of the above

2. Now that we have a supply of black rock, my
   priority should be to:
   a) get the T.O.M. started
   b) get the T.O.M. started
   c) heal that blister on my toe
   d) get the T.O.M. started

Later

Lily kept the flood going for about an hour, long enough for everyone to get their fill. In hindsight, it's lucky that Boris did all that advertising for his Fever Reliever. Black Potion for White Fever! Townspeople needed no prompting. Now sickrooms have gone back to being bedrooms, hospitals are emptying out, and doctors are taking long-overdue nap breaks. Am thankful the stuff works so fast.

Anyway, my fifteen minutes of being concerned about a townful of strangers is fast expiring, and I am ITCHING to put some of this dark elixir to use in time travel. Have filled up a canteen with it. Lily and I are about to head over to Boris' caravan to see about my Time-Out Machine.

Later
DREADFUL SETBACK!!!!!

I have my T.O.M., I have dark elixir, but I am STILL stuck in the eighteenth century.

Yes. Horrible. Unbelievable. I don't understand it, but it seems Lily's dark elixir is NOT Aunt Emma's black rock, and it's not powering my machine.

Am unbearably discouraged!

Here's what happened: No one was at the caravan. We think Boris and his men are most likely back at Lily's house, trying to bottle up some Black Potion. Anyway, that gave us the chance to break in quietly and try to get the Time-Out Machine started. I'd searched my pockets, spreading out all my assorted doodads, knickknacks, thingamabobs, and trinkets on the floor, and analyzed them for possible time travel usefulness. Here's a representative sample of what I found:

1. House key to Dumchester house.
2. House key to Ridicaville house.
3. House key to Tootleston house.
4. House key to Blandindulle house.
5. Assorted paper clips. Not purchased in Duntzton, more's the pity.
6. Assorted slingshotting rocks. All collected in locales other than Duntzton.
7. Slingshot. Built circa my Dumchester days, with various mods circa my Ridicaville and Blandindulle days.
8. Various hood ornaments found on streets of Silifordville, Ridicaville, et al.
9. Loose change.
10. Can of black spray paint I've had at least since Tootleston.
11. Spare cat collar, dating back a year or more.
12. Charm bracelet Mom received at her 13th birthday party.
13. D string from Johnny Ramone's guitar.

Most of these would get me back to the twenty-first century, but NONE had a hope of taking me to the time and place I'd left.

Would be nice if I had actually made myself a copy of Mom's Duntzton house key.

Or saved my receipt from Wilson's Hardware, Antiques, and What-Not.

Or procrastinated a little more on returning Said Student's ID.

Or brought ANY kind of durable, inedible relic of modern-day Duntzton with me.

Oh how I miss that apple!!!!

But I would have to deal with that

problem later. Could not afford to sit around Boris' caravan moping. What I urgently needed at the moment was to see if the T.O.M. would work at all. I reached over to Lily and yanked a single hair from her head before she could even blink in surprise. Put it in the slot, loaded the hopper with Black Potion, spun the dial back in time, hit GO, and crossed my fingers . . .

NO DICE!

AM DOOMED TO DIE BEFORE I AM EVER BORN!!!!!!!

Later

I like the new person that Lily has become, but I'm also a little afraid of her.

She didn't seem at all perturbed when I told her my tragic news. Like I said, she is a new person, without the doubt and helplessness of the old Lily. "Let's get your machine back to the warehouse," was all she said, then helped me heft it onto my back and schlep it out of the caravan.

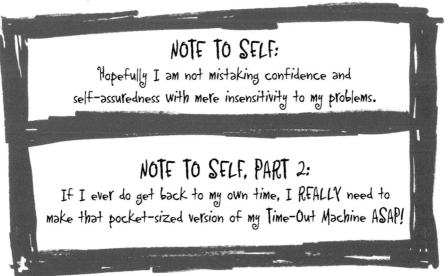

NOTE TO SELF:
Hopefully I am not mistaking confidence and self-assuredness with mere insensitivity to my problems.

NOTE TO SELF, PART 2:
If I ever do get back to my own time, I REALLY need to make that pocket-sized version of my Time-Out Machine ASAP!

When we got back to the warehouse, Lily cleared us all out of her way, then raised her arms gracefully, bringing a small-ish geyser of black rock up from the floor, to be suspended in space like a large black bubble. She stood there with this bubble for a while, patting it with her hands, muttering to herself, and occasionally doing some kind of interesting shimmy. Eventually she called me over. "Go ahead and take some," she told me. "See if that will work for you."

It DID work.

Which is why I'm writing this from some paper-clip manufacturing plant somewhere in the twenty-first century.

Am glad it's the middle of the night, or I'd be drawing some very unwanted attention!

Am breathing HUGE sighs of relief that I can at least get back to my own century. Still no clue how to return to my home in Duntzton, but I tell ya, after a week spent in the 1790s, anything a LITTLE closer to my own time seems downright heavenly.

OK, I should really be heading back to 1790 Seasidetown now. I admit I am a little reluctant to return!!! Am reminding myself that I have unfinished business there. Must make sure Attikol is never able to track down descendants of Lily's family. Must quiz Lily on details of summoning black rock. Must concoct suitable comeuppance for that clabbering Caleb!

All right, here I go. Am using a hangnail pulled off Lily's finger to get myself there. Kind of gross, but I didn't want to take any chances.

Later

Lily and the cats and I are in the tunnel just outside her basement, where Boris and what seem to be his two remaining henchmen are standing around arguing. Their conversation is going a little bit like this:

BORIS:	You mean to tell me that you only filled one bottle before the flow dried up?
MUSKET MAN:	In truth, that bottle is mostly full of mud.
THUGLY:	It's not our fault, Sir Boss. No sooner had we arrived than the black potion began to disappear into the ground. It was almost as though the ground were sucking it up before our eyes!
LILY:	[Silently nodding in satisfaction.]
B:	Joitheads! Fawning clotpoles! Footlickers! Moldwarps! Crusty-eyed gorbellied logger-headed maggot pies!
ME:	[Silently scribbling all this down word for word. Priceless!]

Later

We waited until they left, then cautiously went upstairs to see how Pearl and Opal were doing. Aside from being hungry and anxious, they are fine. No one knows where Caleb is, though. I wanted to tell Opal everything I'd heard Boris say about her beloved psychic, and ask her whether she truly wanted to marry the guy, and suggest that, if so, she should really look into developing a psychic talent of her own so they could have a more two-way communication going, but decided to hold my tongue when I saw how worried she was about him.

We shared what was pretty much the last of Pearl's food stash; then Lily and I went off to her room. I REALLY needed to have a straight talk with her about her new skills with the dark elixir (and what they might, potentially, mean for me and my own source of black rock).

Here's what she had to say:

LILY: You heard the story of how I first came to use the dark elixir for healing. Opal was deathly ill, and I panicked. I had a sort of mental flash—a sort of vision, you might say. I could sense the <u>personality</u> of the elixir for the first time, and that's when I knew it could heal.

ME: And what about when Boris started selling it, and the flow died? Did you do that?

L: Yes, I'm sure of it now.

ME: And the mud in the tunnel? Was that you too?

L: Yes, I believe your training was starting to work!

But I didn't realize it until today. Today, I made real contact with the essence of my elixir. Today, I learned to TALK to the elixir. And to direct it intentionally, not unconsciously.

ME: [SOOO excited.] What was it like? How'd you figure it out?

L: When I felt Enigma's heart stop, I thought I might die with her. Cousin Emily, I think you understand—she's more than a pet, more like . . . part of me! It was like that panic when Opal was ill, only . . . well . . .

ME: [Understanding.] Even stronger. I know. Don't worry, I won't tell your sister.

L: And then, well, I've always been good at following instructions. And Sweetie-Pie told me to start it. So I did. I reached out with my mind to that empty fountain at home, and just . . . started it.

ME: So, at that moment, it was easy?

L: Effortless! Because the dark elixir . . . it's also part of me, in a way.

ME: [Taking notes as fast as possible.] OK, all right, this is good stuff, very helpful, just hope it doesn't take Mystery's near death to start up MY black rock . . .

L: [Very benevolent.] You'll learn how when the time comes. After all, you're a Dark Girl. It's PART of you.

ME: [Feeling totally put in my place as Junior Dark Girl.] [Basically OK with that.] Thanks, Great-Aunt Lily.

Later

Have told Lily everything I heard Boris say about Caleb: how Boris knows I'm here, how Caleb told him about Lily's growing power over the dark elixir, how he seems to have been behind the catnapping and bloodletting. Lily apparently wants to ignore the clear signs of betrayal, though. She says she believes in Caleb no matter what, and she's sure I will come to feel the same. Personally, I don't trust the guy as far as I could drop-kick him, but will just wait and see what happens. Am extremely glad I took the time to learn self-hypnosis and create that psychic barrier before meeting him! Will be tucking WAY more thoughts in that mental hidey-hole before this is over!

Later

We are in a holding pattern, waiting to see if Caleb or Boris will show up, and/or trying to figure out our next move. Am trying to ease my anxiety with some nice calming code-breaking. So far the mysterious letters have not yielded anything interesting, though I was able to make a few intriguing (though unimpressive) anagrams from them:

NL LC AV MA MF EM MK CU AM ME

Ummmmmm lava necklace f
Male uncle mamma vmfmmkc
Manacle muck flame vmmm
Menace mammal luck fmmv

Drat all those Ms!
Amm stummped.

Later

No end to the anxiety, man. Am now feeling uneasy about just how much I've managed to alter history with all this running around, putting mosquito fish in the water supply, talking up germ theory, etcetera, etcetera.

I think I've kind of been overlooking the whole parallel universe danger of time travel. I know it's important to be careful what I change while I'm back in time—and at the very least, to make sure that I return to my own universe and not some weird alternate version of reality that I accidentally created while I was gone.

For example: Maybe some bacteria hop off your skin into the Jurassic, or you leave a cell phone in the nineteenth century, or you give some loser a few innocent stock tips . . . ye olde chaos butterfly flaps its wings, and the Eiffel Tower falls down . . .

and then you go home to a world where you were never born, or people brush their teeth with dirt, or the centipedes are the new ruling class. Now, I'm the first to admit that's entertaining, but really, most of the time I just want to go back to the comforts of home, where my mom, golem, spiders, dead great-aunt, and cats know my name. Luckily, Mom is a tolerant, understanding, fun-loving GOOD SPORT, and can always be relied on for snappy, honest answers to apparently stupid questions like "Hey, Patti, what's my name? Are we still mammals? Who's the President of the United States these days?"

So yeah. Up until this trip, I've been lucky. But I've never spent this long in the past before, let alone changed this much, and right now I'm starting to feel like every move I make, every hair that falls from my head, every molecule of air that's altered because I breathed it in is creating new worlds of infinite divergent contingencies, and I will be bouncing from one to another for all eternity, never finding the one I know . . .

Have to stop thinking of infinite parallel worlds. Am bringing on severe attack of apeirophobia.

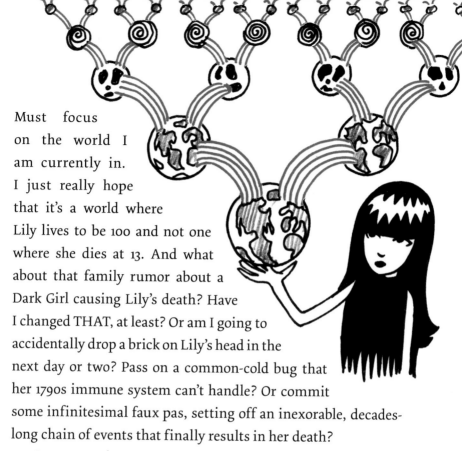

Must focus on the world I am currently in. I just really hope that it's a world where Lily lives to be 100 and not one where she dies at 13. And what about that family rumor about a Dark Girl causing Lily's death? Have I changed THAT, at least? Or am I going to accidentally drop a brick on Lily's head in the next day or two? Pass on a common-cold bug that her 1790s immune system can't handle? Or commit some infinitesimal faux pas, setting off an inexorable, decades-long chain of events that finally results in her death?

GAHHHHH! So many possible Deaths of Lily. So many ways this could all go wrong.

Later

Caleb is back, acting very pleased with himself. Here's what he SAYS he's been up to:

1. Having been monitoring my thoughts and Lily's while we

were out and about,[52] he was well aware of the plight of the Ebenezers, the saga of the flying mosquito fish, and the epic summoning of the dark elixir.

2. He hated to think that Boris might somehow turn the flood of Black Potion to his own advantage.

3. And he decided that it was time for him to do what he could to strike a blow against Boris in his own way.

4. So he paid a visit to the mayor, whom he had met while accompanying Boris to a formal dinner and political gala.

5. And told the mayor a complicated tissue of lies, cleverly interspersed with allusions to the mayor's own private thoughts, that has pretty much ruined Boris' welcome in Seasidetown. Not to mention his ability to sell Black Potion.

6. For example: Was the mayor aware that Boris was actually responsible for bringing the white fever into town?

7. And that, contrary to what the ignorant townspeople might think, the Black Potion was next to useless? (Of course, Caleb was armed with a bottle of Boris' suspiciously moleasses-y potion to prove this point.)

8. Superior minds like the mayor's, of course, would understand that plagues like the white fever could not be cured with the sham medicines of common quacks.

9. And that indeed the answer could be found in the

52 Dratting joithead psychics and their no respect for privacy!

teachings of the ancient Romans and Andalusians:[53] Disease came from tiny creatures, too small to see, carried (in this case) by mosquitoes.

10. But of COURSE, the mayor already knew THAT. Why, any child understood it!

11. Specifically, three children—James, Matthew, and Sweetie-Pie Ebenezer, who happened to be waiting in the foyer with presents of flying mosquito fish, and stories of their success in ridding the town of mosquitoes, and thus the dread white fever.

12. The mayor, who is not at all a superior mind, never noticed he was being steamrolled, but happily thanked Caleb for introducing him to such enterprising, civic-minded young people, statues of whom he promised to have commissioned within a week.

13. And as for Boris, let's just say it would be unwise of him to show his face at the next mayoral soirée.

Hmph. Caleb clearly knows all my reasons for mistrusting him, and is trying some damage control. I gotta give it to him, he knows how to hit some of my soft spots: A) education on disease vectors and mosquito control, B) preservation of the secret of the dark elixir's special qualities, C) future social embarrassment for

---

53 Teachings that he found in MY mind. Habberflacking psychics and their lazy research habits!

Boris, and D) statues of my friends.

Assuming this all actually happened, of course.[54]

And he will still have to answer for the catnapping, bloodletting, and informing Boris of my presence. But I'm not going to challenge him openly, in front of Opal and Pearl—I'm sure they would react just like Lily did. No, my suspicions are between me and Caleb. Have sent him a very clear psychic memo to the effect that I am watching him closely, and with serious misgivings!

Later

Back in Lily's room. Trying to lay the foundation for a nice solid plan that will hide Lily and her dark elixir from Boris forever. Am taking inspiration from A) the Original Death of Lily by White Fever, and B) protagonists through the ages who needed to make someone stop chasing them for all time. In other words, we're going to fake Lily's death!!!! So simple. So effective. In fact, the more I think about it, the more I'm deciding that I may have been a bit misled in thinking that various possible Deaths of Lily happen in various Separate Universes. I think that, actually, A) Lily IS going to die of white fever (without being bitten by any mosquitoes, or suffering any symptoms), AND B) Lily is going to fake her death to get rid of Boris, AND C) a Dark Girl is indeed going to cause Lily's death (well, OK, her FAKE death), all in this

---

54 I will be doing some fact-checking with James, Matthew, and Sweetie-Pie, you bet your cheeks!!!

178

exact universe I'm in right here and now.

Have created a Venn diagram to explain my hypothesis. Am sure to receive extra credit from Mom for this!

How neat and tidy. The history Aunt Millie taught me actually depended on me to come back here and create it.

—Jeez, what if I hadn't felt like coming?

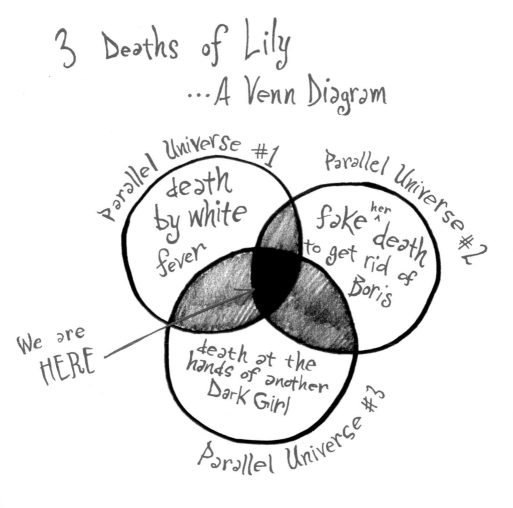

3 Deaths of Lily
...A Venn Diagram

Parallel Universe #1
death by white fever

Parallel Universe #2
fake her death to get rid of Boris

We are HERE

death at the hands of another Dark Girl

Parallel Universe #3

Anyway. Lily and I have done some planning. Here's what we've come up with:

1. Lily is going straight to bed with a severe (severely FAKE!) case of white fever.
2. Caleb will bring Boris to come see her.
3. And she'll plead with him for that last muddy bottle of Black Potion, claiming to be too far gone to summon any herself.
4. He may or may not give it to her, but either way, her condition's not going to improve any.
5. And at the critical moment, we'll administer a dose of paramytosilicate extract—100% deathlike effect, every time!
6. Paramytosilicate extract that I will have retrieved from my bedroom back in Tootleston, having used my house key to jump there.[55]
7. Once Boris has seen her lifeless body, Caleb will get him occupied in planning her funeral.
8. During which time I will get the entire family safely hidden in the warehouse.
9. Then Caleb, Pearl, Lily, and Opal will escape in the funeral coach that Boris himself will hire for them.
10. Now that the mayor is about to declare Seasidetown free

---

55 Man, I LOOOOOVE those times when it pays to be a pack rat!

Étrange

of white fever, they should have no problem getting to Salem, where they can take refuge at Caleb's parents' home.

11. Then I'll say my farewells to Seasidetown and the Ebenezers.

12. And zap myself and Mystery back to my own time using . . . hmmmm . . . well, using something yet to be determined.

13. Then go tell Mom and Aunt Millie how it all REALLY happened.

Later—MUCH later

Lily and I are back in the twenty-first century! I had no intention of taking her with me! She was sitting there so innocently on her bed back in 1790 Seasidetown, just watching me load up the Time-Out Machine's hopper with dark elixir and drop my Tootleston house key into the slot, and I guess I was too absorbed in my calibrations with the selection dial to notice her creeping closer and closer to the machine, curiosity and eager sense of adventure burning in her eyes. At the last moment before I hit GO, she and Enigma jumped in with me.[56] Moldwarps! They had better not make any trouble here. This is

---

56 Am now feeling the consequences of training Great-Aunt Lily in self-confidence!

MY history, and I don't want any changes!

Grrr. Anyway: We landed in the backyard of my Tootleston house. Could be better, could be worse; at least it's daytime, so my Tootleston self is asleep, and the fence is high, so no one is likely to see Lily or the T.O.M. I made her swear up and down she would behave, then Mystery and I slipped in through a window and commenced to sneakin'.

Later

Back outside. I got the stuff. It was a very creepy experience breaking into my own bedroom, disarming my own booby traps, finding MY OWN SELF sound asleep under my own four cats, tiptoeing around them, trying not to breathe. I grabbed the extract and split. Tried to shake off the whole mind-bending, queasy experience. Do not like encountering myself in journeys

to the past. Way too many possibilities for Parallel Universe Danger. Way too much temptation to sit down and have a chat with myself about all the trouble I can avoid down the road if I will just listen to my future self for a moment. Yeah. My mind hurts to think of all the additional trouble THAT would surely get me into.

At least Lily more or less behaved herself while I was gone. She passed the time staring through a knothole in the fence at a busy sidewalk in a world 200+ years later than her own. Needless to say, she had some questions for me.

And Now, Emily Explains to 1790s Girl . . .

1. Trousers on Females
2. Facial Piercing
3. The Cellular Telephone
4. The Mullet
5. Short Shorts
6. Green Hair Dye
7. Iced-Out Grillz
8. Moon Boots
9. Tube Tops
10. Skateboards
11. Text Messaging
12. The Purse Dog
13. Bling

Later—or earlier?

Oh boy. Lily and I are NOT in Seasidetown, 1790. No, we are in Manhattan, 1974—the Ramones' first show. I know, probably not the smartest plan, but Lily seemed so interested in the concept of punk, which really is best explained with examples. She is a little bit blown away, I think. Mostly by the volume—a decibel level completely unknown in the 1790s, I can tell you. Her pristine eardrums are getting a workout tonight! Both cats are cowering in the Time-Out Machine, pissed off at us. Maybe we'll stay for one more number and roll out. The next song is only forty-two seconds long, anyway. Man, I never get tired of seeing this show.

OK, Lily is already attracting some interested glances from fashionista types. Don't want to change the history of Young Ladies' Apparel too drastically if I can help it.[57]

Later

We are in my bedroom in Blandindulle. I finally let Lily talk me into allowing her into my home. One of my homes, anyway. My past self is off on that journey to Great-Aunt Emma's house in Blackrock, allowing plenty of time for my current self to show Lily around my Blandindulle bedroom. I showed Lily the Oddisee, the Tilt-A-Girl™, and that computer I made out of Lincoln Logs. She actually seemed to understand pretty well how it worked. I had to stop her enthusiastic adulation of my genius

---

57 Would also like to avoid my Blandindulle self, who is standing a couple yards away with her back to me.

by explaining how much I crowd-surfed on the shoulders of others to make that thing.[58]

She's been perusing my bookshelves and music collection. And Now, Emily Explains to 1790s Girl . . .

1. M.C. Escher
2. <u>Finnegans Wake</u>
3. The Residents
4. <u>Waka/Jawaka</u>
5. <u>Ziggy Stardust and the Spiders from Mars</u>
6. <u>My Cousin, My Gastroenterologist</u>
7. Gwar
8. <u>Quadrophenia</u>
9. The New York Dolls
10. <u>Metal Machine Music</u>
11. Dead Kennedys
12. Jackson Pollock
13. <u>Pride and Prejudice and Zombies</u>

Later

We are about to leave Blandindulle, but first, we are going to sneak a quick peek at my mom, since Lily seems to have her heart set on seeing at least one member of my family. It is totally ill advised, but Lily has this new, authoritative Elder Dark Aunt way about her now, and I'm having trouble saying no.

---

58 Anyway, it's really only good for playing solitaire.

Later

It was actually very gratifying to slink into Mom's bedroom so that Lily could "meet" her. Like me, Lily has met very few relatives (in fact, most of the relatives I'VE met have, technically, been long dead), so it was kind of a special moment.

> LILY: [Eyes misting up.] She's beautiful! I can't wait to tell Pearl and Opal all about her. And what about your siblings? Do you have sisters? Brothers?
>
> ME: Can't help you there, Lily. No siblings. None that I know of, anyway.
>
> LILY: [Pausing to consider what it said about one's parents if one considered secret siblings a distinct possibility.] What a world you live in, Cousin Emily.

Later/earlier/later/etc.

OK—Lily and I may be on a bit of a bender here with the time travel. I keep sort of gently suggesting that we head back to 1790, but Lily keeps producing interesting artifacts she obviously lifted from my Blandindulle bedroom, then summoning these huge bubbles of dark elixir . . . and, well, who I am to argue with my Auntie? We have hit Paris, 1977; Berkeley, 1967; Shanghai, 1127; Eridu, 5007 BC; Reykjavik, 877; Kathla'amat, 1377; Los Angeles, 1947; and Dubai, 2007—where we are now. I am getting overwhelmed with it all, we have been carrying two very exhausted

cats on our shoulders for the past five stops, and I suspect Lily may be hitting her limit soon. Suspect and HOPE!

Later/earlier, again

We are back in Lily's bedroom, 1790. Longest day of our lives. Time for bed!

Saturday, August 14, 1790

Today's assignments:
- Serious code-breaking (LATE!!)—1/3 points
- Enact Grand Scheme to Thwart Boris Forever—13/3 points

Opal and Pearl woke us up in the late afternoon. I think they had the best intentions of letting us sleep in until sundown, but we had left them piles of delectable Foodstuffs From the Ages (OK, mostly from the Blandindulle supermarket), and they could not hold back their extravagant gratitude any longer.

> PEARL: Asparagus! Asparagus in August, Lily! It's like sorcery!
>
> OPAL: And those chocolate confections with the creamy center! The ones wrapped in very thin metal! I thought I would expire with pleasure!
>
> ME: [Groggy.] Yes. There's nothing quite like your very first artificial sugar high. Hey, it must be about time for us to put on our show for Boris, right?

Later

Plan is in motion. Caleb is with Boris in the caravan, ready to alert him once Lily is prepared. Man, I hope we can trust him. Opal and Pearl have hidden all anachronistic foodstuffs and made a pretty passable sickroom out of Lily's bedroom. We have decorated Lily's face with beads of sugary icing—brilliant effect! And the paramytosilicate extract is in Pearl's pocket, all ready to deal Lily her fake-death blow, and destroy Boris' dreams of Black Potion Power once and for all!

Later

I'm hiding in the attic with the cats. Boris is downstairs with Lily. Sure wish I could hear what's going on. Heavy footsteps, some raised voices—that's about all I can make out. Please, please let him believe she is dying!

Later

Clotpoles! The plan seems to have gone horribly awry! Pearl and Opal are in hysterics. Boris has taken Lily away!!! Here's a rough re-enactment I dragged out of Opal and Pearl:

BORIS: You! Blasted fawning dewberry of a woman! Why did you not summon me earlier?

PEARL: But . . . she only just fell ill . . .

B: Clearly, she is not safe in your care. I shall take her

	to my caravan, where I can stand watch over her myself.
P:	No! Oh, Cousin Boris, I pray you, do not remove my child!
B:	Be silent, you clay-brained featherhead! I shall send for the finest doctor in town and return your daughter when she recovers. IF she recovers.

Pearl never had a chance to give Lily the extract. Caleb is not around—he didn't arrive with Boris like he promised to. Opal is freaking out that something has happened to him. As for me, I am feeling a complete renewal of my ugly suspicions about Caleb's role in all this. I KNEW we shouldn't have trusted him to help with our plans! How do we know his loyalties aren't really with Boris? As for what he says he told the mayor, well, I have absolutely no proof that he even SAW the mayor! And now I'm thinking back to the day he menaced me in the hall, and reflecting that if I were as psychic as Caleb, I'd be in a perfect position to play both sides off each other, and be the only one benefiting from the whole mess. Well, not if I can help it. The cats and I are off to the caravan!

Later

Am under the caravan. AGAIN. With the paramytosilicate extract in my pocket, the 1790s outfit on, Mystery and Enigma by my side, and the chamber-pot trapdoor open just a crack, so that I can hear what's going on inside. Boris definitely seems to have called a doctor in to see Lily. I really can't tell if this doctor sounds competent at all. He's been talking on and on about miasmas and humors—no hint of bloodletting yet. If I hear any mention of that, I'm just going to have to bust in and let the chips fall where they may!

Two minutes later

He has mentioned bloodletting. Here I go—

MUCH later

So much has happened! I hardly know where to start. Will just chronicle events as they occurred. Let's see—oh yeah, bloodletting. I did not really stop to think at all, but rode my sense of panic right up through that trapdoor and into the caravan. There was Lily, stretched out on a bunk, eyes closed, playing sick; there was (I assumed) the doctor, with his terrifying (and totally nonsterile) lancet poised over my aunt's innocent arm, hunting for a vein; there was Boris, sitting behind the doctor, looking angry and anxious; there was Caleb, gagged and tied to a chair (interesting, but I'd have to come back to that later, as I had a vein to save).

So I popped up out of the floor. That's really all I did. The doctor saw me, shrieked, and fled into the night, knocking Boris over in his hurry to get away from the horrible apparition. Boris' chair went over backward, and I heard a thump as his head hit something hard. I went up closer to get a look at him—out cold. I locked the caravan door, just in case Musket Man and Thugly were around, and turned my attention to Caleb, who was gazing at me with pleading eyes. I unfolded my pocketknife and approached him.

I can be kinda psychic in my own way too, and I could plainly see what he was thinking—he knew all my suspicions, and everything I'd heard Boris say. He knew I still wanted my revenge on him for the menacing; he knew how easy it would be for me to slide that knife between his ribs or across his windpipe, and tell Opal it had been Boris. —Hmph. I decide whom to avenge myself on, and when! I cut him loose, of course. Murder's not my style. But I let him know pretty clearly that I'd get him some other time, when he least expected it.

CALEB: Thank you, Miss Emily. I swear on . . . I swear on my love for Miss Opal, you can trust me completely.

ME: Oh, well, we'll see about that. First tell me why you're tied up like this!

C: Boris lost his temper completely when he heard that Lily had fallen ill. Furthermore, he has the patience of a mosquito, and blames me for failing to help him obtain the black potion.

ME: OK, any thoughts on the current mess?

C: Certainly! To start with, Boris never saw you there before the doctor knocked him over. Perhaps you'll find it advisable to hide again before he revives.

ME: Why bother? He knows I'm around. You just HAD to tell him, didn't you?

C: Yes, I DID have to tell him. The one you call Musket Man had already seen you and was soon to tell Boris himself.

ME: WHAT? How did he see me?

C: Oh, they have a peephole into Pearl's room.

ME: Oh. I see.

C: However, you bring up a salient point. He knows of your presence and will likely pursue you, unless . . .

E: [Suspecting where this was going.] Unless . . .

C: Unless you're dead.

ME: You know, it would be a LITTLE easier for me to believe you if you didn't SAY things like that.

C: I think you may have some trust issues, Miss Emily.

ME: Now where would a 1790s guy have encountered a phrase like "trust issues"?

C: [Innocently.] The same place I encountered "Evil Overlord of the Universe," "dratting joithead psychic," and "Metal Machine Music."

ME: [Grrrr . . .] OK . . . but I only have enough extract for one dose.

C: Then you must pretend! I will tell Boris you came here of your own initiative to see the doctor, but your case of white fever was too advanced, and the sight of your departed cousin caused you to perish in shock. He'll believe it, I assure you.

ME: OK then, I'm just going to give Lily her dose . . . it'll make her appear dead for about three hours. And I guess I'll just have to fake it as long as I can. Hey, Lily, how ya doing there? That was great, staying in character through all that, but you can open your eyes now. . . Uh, Aunt Lily?

That's when Caleb and I discovered that Lily was actually unconscious.

ME: What did that doctor do before I got here? WHAT DID HE DO TO HER????

CALEB: Well, he stood over her, talking about bloodletting, waving his lancet around! Any young lady would faint under circumstances such as those!

ME: Not real big on girl power, are you, Caleb?

I've read enough eighteenth-century literature to know how to revive a young lady from a faint. But seeing as I was fresh out of smelling salts and mulled wine, and not really knowing what it means to chafe someone's hands, I settled for some light slapping and poking. Eventually her eyes opened.

LILY: Is that awful doctor gone?

ME: Long gone. Are you ready to die? It won't hurt a bit—and we'll all be waiting for you on the other side . . . of the, uh, nap, I mean. Sorry, I just always wanted to say that.

L: I'm ready! [Catching sight of Caleb. Gushing.] Oh, Caleb . . . I saw Cousin Emily's mother, Patricia. She has your mouth—and Opal's chin!

CALEB: Errrr??—Oh. My goodness. Isn't that interesting, Miss Emily?

ME: [Light dawning.] Uhhhhh . . . VERY interesting!

C: [Laughing. Very pleased with himself.] I suppose that makes me your great-great-grandfather, doesn't it?

ME: Probably more like ten or twelve "greats," but yeah, it looks that way.

C: Well, then, I'm going to expect a little more respect and obedience out of you, in that case.

ME: Why, you—oh. Ha. Ha. Yes. You got me. The old intergenerational humor barrier.

C: In all seriousness, Miss Emily, would you mind tying me up again before Boris recovers?

Good gobfarx. How downright SLOW of me not to have pieced THAT together before now. OF COURSE Opal and Caleb are my direct ancestors! That Diabolical Revenge I was so looking forward to wreaking on Caleb will now need to be dialed down to Family-Style Payback—still a bit stronger than Cat-Specific Comeuppance in my personal hierarchy of vengeances, but milder than Just-for-Fun Retaliation. Oh well. Will console myself by making Caleb's revenge an exercise in retribution style points.

Oh. And another thing. I don't think I'm too far off the mark to suppose that Caleb and Opal are most likely Jakey's ancestors as well! Will have to make sure to call him Cousin next time I see him.

—Anyway, back to the story—

I retied Caleb, dosed Lily, gave the cats strict instructions to stay hidden under the bed until further notice, and got myself all laid out in fake death next to Lily before Boris woke up. There

Our glorious fake death scene!

was a lot of groaning, followed by a loud scream of horror, followed by a lot of swearing, followed by a loud temper tantrum, followed by loud questions directed at Caleb, followed by the apparent untying of Caleb's gag, followed by Caleb's soothing voice as he attempted to calm Boris down. I had never witnessed Caleb actually talking to Boris before. Wow . . . I really didn't realize just how tightly Caleb has Boris wound around his finger! I wonder if Jakey does the same with Attikol?

Here are the high points of their conversation (translated from 1790s English):

1. Caleb convinced Boris that he had fainted at the sight of Miss Lily's tragic death at the hands of the doctor.

2. Then he spun a brilliant web of lies concerning my arrival (alas, too late for treatment) and subsequent death.

3. Boris then launched into a diatribe on why Caleb had

learned nothing of "those witches' secrets" during his time with the Étrange family.

4. Then threatened to dump him off the wharf, still tied to his chair.

5. And announced his intention of dumping my body and Lily's at the mass graves and driving the caravan straight out of town.

6. At which point Caleb made a big show of Revealing Ye Olde Grande Secret, then told Boris the Étrange family's ancestral source of dark elixir, which had finally been made clear to him when Lily was at death's door.

7. Said secret being that dark elixir is formed in the graves of the Étrange family's so-called Dark Girls—namely, me and Lily.

8. So all Boris needed to do was to observe a few simple rituals: first, give me and Lily a properly respectful burial in a safe place (most logically, the basement of Lily's house), and second, say the Words of Dark Summoning over our coffins. Then sit back and wait.

9. Furthermore, there was really no need to keep Pearl and Opal around any longer now that Lily was dead. Naturally, they'd need to be "taken care of" as well.

10. Needless to say, my guts were churning with fear and distrust as I was listening to all this!

11. And I was pretty much resigning myself to being buried alive, if not killed outright, especially when Caleb told Boris where he could find the last two coffins left in Seasidetown.
12. Said coffins having been reserved by the town coffin maker for himself and his wife.
13. But Caleb, boasting of his ability to see inside every mind in town, assured Boris that the coffin maker believed the plague was over, and was ready to sell.

And with that, Caleb hurried out on his grim errand.

Leaving me alone with my evil Uncle Boris and my unconscious Great-Aunt Lily.

I listened in anxiety and fear for a while as Boris scratchy-scratched at something on his desk. Had no idea what he was doing until I had a bit of an insight into yet another thing Boris and I have in common: the journal-writing habit. OF COURSE he was chronicling all this so that, unbeknownst to him, his Great[10]-Grandson Attikol could one day read it . . . and use it to track ME down.

Oh wait a flamdrabbling minute.

Wasn't my plan supposed to do something to prevent that possibility?

But I hadn't achieved that at all. I'd been so caught up in

making the Three Deaths of Lily coincide, I'd overlooked the need to hide Opal and Pearl (and therefore, their descendants . . . and therefore, ME) for all time.

It looked like that was going to be OK, though . . . because Caleb was apparently taking care of that for me, with the (hopefully fake) deaths of Opal and Pearl.

At least, I seriously hoped that was the case. Of course, if he was actually going to have them killed, I'd never be born, and wouldn't be in much condition to care.

Ages passed . . . Well, OK, seriously, like two hours. I was starting to get a bit anxious about the paramytosilicate extract wearing off before Lily was safely buried. And, I'll admit it, my eyes were getting a BIT uncomfortable staying open that long. (Didn't I mention? I'd decided to be dead with my eyes open.) I mean, I WAS proclaimed Staring Contest Champion of the Hemisphere for three years running . . . but two hours is a long time, even for me.

Ages passed . . . I tried a little mental code-breaking to while away the time. Usually that calms me down like a charm, but this time, well, those dratting Ms kept fouling things up every time I thought I'd come up with something.

Ages passed . . . I started to SERIOUSLY doubt Caleb's intentions of following through with any plan at all. What if he had abandoned us to Boris? Lily would be waking up soon. The lie would be out. And Boris, knowing what he thought he knew

A real sweet ride to the Hereafter.

about the origins of his Black Potion, might decide to REALLY kill Lily this time.

And then, FINALLY, Caleb returned.

He had the coffins—two truly beautiful coffins, which happened to get placed near the foot of the bunk, conveniently within my field of vision. I lay there and just admired them. Those lines, that grain, that depth of color, the sheer artisanship! Man, I've always been kind of a connoisseur of fly-looking coffins, but I don't think I ever saw any that a coffin maker crafted for himself. Those puppies were SICK! Could hardly believe my luck. I was about to be buried in the best-looking coffin I'd ever seen, and I wouldn't even be too dead to enjoy myself.

Caleb and Boris managed to rudely interrupt my reverie by putting Lily in her coffin. Then it was my turn. The lid closed over my face.[59] Boris slammed around the caravan, asking where the hammer was, but Caleb stopped him, offering to nail the lids

59 Flamjarks! It's lucky for me and Lily that embalming wasn't more widespread in 1790!

himself, then convinced Boris to get out and find those thugs of his so they could "take care of" Pearl and Opal.

Anyway, as soon as Boris was gone, Caleb lifted the lids, and I called for the cats to come and get inside the coffins.

ME: OK, Caleb, I hope I can trust you, man. You sure you have a solid plan?

CALEB: Absolutely solid. Your friend John Ebenezer helped me prepare the coffins with false bottoms—see the latch? He has widened the passageway to the tunnel, as well—you will simply drop down into it. You will find your machine there. Use this handkerchief in it. My mother sent it to me just days ago. She wove the fabric herself. It should get you to her home in Salem. Now, don't fear—I'll see it in her mind as soon as you arrive. And if I don't, I'll exhume the coffins myself.

ME: WHAT THE GLAMKINS? Exhume the coffins? You're really going to BURY us?

C: I can think of no way around it! Boris will expect to see you buried, and—

ME: Oh, I wasn't complaining. [Arranging Mystery comfortably at my feet.] [Lying back and folding my hands across my chest.] It's a bit of a dream come true for me. Nail those lids down kind of loose, though. We WILL need air.

C: [Flustered. Maybe a little weirded out.] Never
       fear, Miss Emily, I've tucked breathing straws all
       around the perimeter. I do hope the dirt doesn't
       pack down too tightly around you, though.

So there I was, feeling like the luckiest girl on earth. To be buried
alive in such a majestic coffin! MAJOR life goal achieved!!!!

Eventually Boris and thugs arrived and carried our coffins out
to what was presumably a cart of some kind, because we then had
a jolting ride back to Lily's house. Around then I started to get
fussed about when Lily would wake up. Had I calculated the dos-
age correctly for her weight? Would she wake up before we were
buried, and kick and scream? Or would she wake too late—and
we'd be underground for another hour, slowly running out of air,
until her fake death transitioned seamlessly into her real death?
And I'd be responsible—just like the family rumor said. Caleb
was right to have been suspicious of me—I wasn't handling this
well at all—I couldn't be trusted—!!!

And then I heard a whisper at one of the breathing tubes near
my ear.

CALEB: Keep your nerve, Miss Emily! You'll be in Salem in
        ten minutes or I'll dig you up myself!

Yes. Yes. Relax and enjoy the ride, I told myself. If for some reason
your fake-dead Great[10]-Aunt doesn't revive and break out of her

false-bottomed coffin so that the two of you can time-travel to Salem, Great[10]-Grandpa can always exhume you.[60]

As it turned out, our timing was either excellent or dreadful, depending on how you see it. I heard Lily give a groan just as the men lifted the coffins off the cart. The foot end of my coffin dropped six inches—Boris gave a yelp—but Caleb reassured him, saying all corpses made groaning noises as the air left their bodies. The coffin steadied and they carried us inside to the final resting place—of our beautiful Chariots to the Hereafter. Lily groaned again, but no one seemed to take notice. And then I could hear her stirring, and FLAMDRAB IT, Enigma started to purr—but we were already in the grave, and the dirt was raining down. Oh beauty! I gave myself a brief moment to enjoy it, then took pity on Lily, who was probably a bit freaked out.

ME: [Calling over the noise of dirt falling . . . sending brainwaves to Caleb to start in on his bogus Words of Dark Summoning . . . Nice and loud, Caleb, nice and loud . . .] OK, Lily, hit the latch! . . . Hit the latch, Lily! —ENIGMA, HIT THE LATCH!!!!!

And it worked, it worked, it worked . . .

We slogged through the (QUITE mucky) tunnel to find the Time-Out Machine around the first bend.

60 Oh, man. I LOVE the fact that I can write sentences like that about my family!

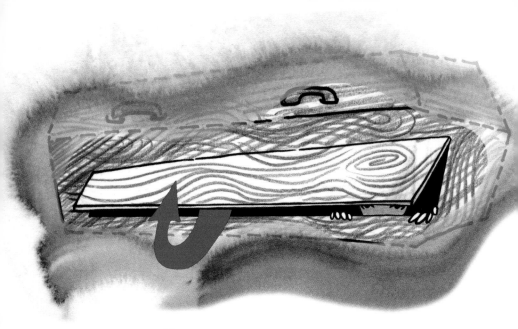

Sunday, August 15, 1790
Today's assignments:
- Thank Caleb for improving on my plan—13 points
- Arrange Family Style Revenge on Caleb for the menacing—113 points

Have successfully avenged myself on Caleb, who I'm pretty sure spent the evening of August 14 frantically digging up two empty coffins, not having gotten any psychic signal from his mother that we'd arrived in her house. That would be the result of this lovely chain of events:

1. While in the coffin, I instructed myself to use my Blandindulle house key in the Time-Out Machine instead of Caleb's handkerchief.

2. Then immediately buried that instruction with a neat little bit of self-hypnosis.
3. Once back in modern-day Blandindulle, Lily and I made our way to my old pal Zenith's Junk Shoppe.
4. And spent a good hour sifting through some Verye Dustye Itemes looking for something that would suit my purposes.
5. E.g., a copy of a Salem newspaper dated August 15, 1790.
6. It turned out that Zenith had no such thing, but he was able to find one online for me.
7. Ordered it.
8. Waited seven days for delivery.[61]
9. Then inserted said newspaper in the T.O.M., and off we went.
10. Scared the spit out of Caleb's parents by materializing in their living room.
11. But, having raised Caleb, they are clearly used to The Weird Stuff, and are coping very well now.
12. By which I mean they are running around getting us

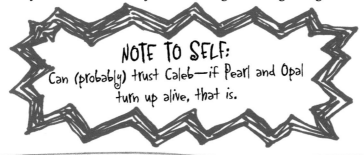

NOTE TO SELF:
Can (probably) trust Caleb—if Pearl and Opal turn up alive, that is.

---

61 That's actually a bit of a lie. We used the T.O.M., of course.

washbasins and towels, savory foodstuffs, and cold drinks.

13. Am still avoiding the cyder. Beverages that smell that much like jet fuel don't cross my lips.

Later

Pretty sure I have never enjoyed daylight hours quite so much. Then again, have never spent daylight hours on a 1790s ranch. I credit the bonnet for making it all possible. Have had a lovely afternoon of relaxing with Lily, the cats, a bunch of crazy chickens, several beautiful horses, and fifty acres of unspoiled wilderness. It's a little like being on vacation at a dude ranch, without all the annoying dudes.

Have also tried my hand again at some code-breaking on those letters. It made me very cross. Had to give up after some fruitless attempts when I found myself making Ws, Ns, and Vs out of all those Ms in desperate effort to force them into some kind of sense. Am giving up and going back out to the horses.

Later

Opal and Pearl have turned up alive! Oh, this is such good news! I guess I will get born after all. It seems John Ebenezer appeared at their house and broke down the front door, then convinced them[62] to lie down in the cart, which he's been using for the past week to haul away dead bodies. He partially covered them with a

---

62 By quoting Caleb's pet name for Opal—"Gem of my heart." Ewwwwww.

horse blanket; then, once Boris and Caleb arrived with the coffins, he made like to drive away. Caleb made a big show of inquiring what on earth he was doing, and John announced that he'd been called in to remove two bodies from the house—the plague's final victims. Caleb dramatically pretended to inspect the bodies, exclaiming in horror at the signs of plague. Boris and thugs were so relieved to be out of the job that they couldn't send the wagon on its way quickly enough.

GOOD STUFF!!!!!!!!!!

Caleb is still outside, tending the horses, but should be in shortly. Am looking forward to his side of the story.

Later

Caleb finally came in, with a special scowl reserved for me. I knew right away it was for the grave-digging. But really he can only blame himself for that. And THAT'S what makes it the best revenge possible. (That, and all the style points I awarded myself.)

Anyway, he has just finished telling us how he enlisted John Ebenezer's help to wrangle the Time-Out Machine through the basement pit into the tunnel, rig the coffins and passageway, and fake Opal and Pearl's deaths. Apparently, once Lily and I were buried and the sham Words of Dark Summoning intoned, Caleb offered to watch the graves for signs of Black Potion while Boris went home to Philadelphia for a well-deserved vacation.

Of course, as soon as Boris was gone, Caleb started to panic. He still hadn't seen anything in his parents' minds about our arrival. Not knowing where any of the other entrances to the tunnel were, and not being able (for once) to raid my brain for easy information, he frantically dug up the coffins—which he found empty.

Hoping that Lily and I would somehow make it safely to Salem, he went to the warehouse and collected Opal and Pearl. Then they made the journey here, with Caleb anxiously scanning the countryside with his mind, looking for us. Midway through their journey (Opal told us), he dropped the reins and screamed—that would have been at the moment my Time-Out Machine landed in his mother's kitchen. AHhahhahaHAHhh! Excellent stuff.

However, I had another issue to settle with Caleb, one that I preferred to discuss in private. I stepped outside, mentally signaling him to follow.

ME: All that's well and good, Caleb, but we both know you have more to explain.

CALEB: You're referring to the catnapping and bloodletting, I assume?

ME: Yeah, were you really behind that? And if so . . . WHAT THE FLABJARX???

C: Yes, I told Boris that pouring the blood of the witch cat into the basement pit would restart the fountain of Black Potion.

ME: Gahhhhh! What were you thinking?

C: Miss Emily, I based my idea on what YOU were thinking. I quote: "The way to inspire Lily's successful summoning is through her tender little heart."

ME: But what if Enigma had actually DIED?

C: Don't forget that Lily's mind is even more an open book to me than yours. I can delve deeper inside it than even Lily can. And what I found there assured me that she would never let Enigma die—that the threat would provoke Lily to rise to her full control over the Black Potion, just as the threat to Opal's health released Lily's healing talent years ago.

ME: Oh . . . kay. I guess you're off the hook, then. —So, hey, my mind's NOT as open of a book, then?

C: [Looking slightly irked.] No, I know of your mental barrier, and have not yet surmounted it. However, I suppose I can hardly grudge you your secrets.

ME: Well, thanks. Oh . . . and thanks for improving on my plan. I mean, killing off Opal and Pearl—good touch! Kind of essential to keeping Boris' descendants off my trail.

211

C: Not at all, Miss Emily. I owe my plan's success entirely to you.

ME: Yeah, I guess all the elements DID come from shameless combing through MY mind . . . but thanks all the same, man. Now listen, I happen to know a young relative of yours in the twenty-first century who could use a little help.

CALEB: You're speaking of Master Jakey, I suppose? Moon Child of the Valley of the Knowing?

ME: That's the kid. Look, Boris is going to be writing in his diary about how his dratting joithead psychic betrayed him and ruined his chances to get his hands on the dark elixir, and . . .

C: And two hundred years later, his descendant will read that diary, and . . .

ME: [Silently/psychically.] It's soooooooo annoying when you do that, dude.

C: My apologies. Please continue, Miss Emily.

ME: Yeah, well, Attikol's got some trust issues of his own. And he's got this kid under tight surveillance because of your hijinks. I'm just saying, it's gonna be a lot easier on Jakey until I can spring him from that medicine show if Boris doesn't end up thinking you betrayed him.

C: So you wish me to stay in Boris' employ?

ME: I just think that a smart, enterprising psychic

might be able to play both sides of the fence and turn the situation to his advantage.

C: I see through the flattery, Miss Emily, but I do feel your point. Very well. I shall return to Boris for the present. Perhaps I will find a more subtle ploy to leave him before my marriage to Miss Opal.

ME: [Generously.] Hey, I've seen a lot of movies, man. Consider my mind your library.

Later

Caleb and I put in an hour of good collaborative planning on how to keep Opal and Pearl out of sight of Boris' family for all time. Have adjusted my mental barrier so that Caleb now has free access to the plots of all the movies and books and TV shows I've ever seen or read, but not to my personal thoughts and secrets. He is sitting around with his mouth open, shaking his head at what he's seeing. Good Stuff!

Now Opal is clamoring for Caleb to come and help her plan their wedding. Am going outside with Lily for Quality Horse Time.

Monday, August 16, 1790

Today's assignments:

- Find perfect wedding gift for 1790s couple—13 points
- Devise return route to the Duntzton I left—113 points

So I bid my relatives adieu, accepting little packages of hominy to go, invitations to Opal and Caleb's wedding, and handkerchiefs freshly embroidered with my initials and Patti's.

Then Mystery and I zipped back to Seasidetown one last time. I really wanted to see the Ebenezers again. They weren't in the warehouse, but they'd left me a note with their new address. The mayor has given them one of the city's many empty houses. John has gone back to his regular job at the wharves, which are being prepped to reopen tomorrow. But I found Hannah and the kids at home, and spent the afternoon hanging out with them, seeing all Meryl's latest tricks, enjoying Hannah's home cooking—1000% better than her warehouse cooking. You know, good times. Also—have had a long talk with Hannah about Sweetie-Pie. Get this! It turns out that Hannah's family has its own line of unusually talented girls. They humbly call them Bright Girls. Can you believe that? I mean, I can. It would be pretty arrogant of me to assume that my family's the only one in the world with . . . well, you know. Special qualities. Sweetie-Pie's from a different mold, all right, but still. It's good to know there's more of us out there.

Later

Have figured out my return route home. Here's how it goes:

1. Visit Lily's house—more specifically, her garden—and fill my pockets with cuttings from some of these incredible plants.
2. Head to the 21st century via my Dumchester house key.
3. Hide the T.O.M. in my backyard in Dumchester.
4. Take a bus the 27 miles to Duntzton and locate the house that Mom and I would eventually move into, years down the road.
5. Plant the cuttings in the backyard of said house.
6. Camp out in said backyard for the 43 hours it takes for said cuttings to form roots and establish themselves as viable plants.
7. Take cuttings of said cuttings.
8. Take a bus the 27

miles back to Dumchester.

9. Reflect for the millionth time how much I need to build myself that pocket-sized T.O.M.
10. Return to T.O.M. and place 2nd-generation cuttings in the slot.
11. Fill hopper with black rock.
12. Pick random spot on dial— plenty of time for fine-tuning when I land in Duntzton!
13. Press GO.

It might not be the most direct route home, but I give it extra credit for style.

Sunday, October 23, 1790

Today's assignment:
- Return to my own familiar universe—infinity points!!!!!

Opal and Caleb had a beautiful wedding, as weddings go. They had it at night in respect for Lily's nocturnal lifestyle. The best part, of course, was seeing Lily and Enigma again, although for me it's only been a couple of hours since I saw them last.

Opal's wedding, before things got disgustingly gushy.

Lily had a going-away present for me: this vast crock of black rock. It was touching, and believe me I was tempted, but I can't go through life using other Dark Girls' dark elixir. I gracefully declined. She understood.

Am headed home!!!!!!!!

Sept. 7 (second time)

Today's assignments:

- Assemble new PrimevilPowerCase®—13 points
- Get quality time with cats—53 points
- Make sure I am back in the same world I left— 1313 points

Back at home! Oh, it is so good to be home! Mystery and I have had a very sweet rasslin' with Miles, Sabbath, and NeeChee, who were not at all pleased to be woken up, as they just saw us an hour ago. Too bad. I have missed them and they are getting a good rasslin' to make up for it.

Raven went "Uhhhhhhhh . . . hey" at me with her normal level of enthusiasm. Told her to rearrange my record collection as a test command. Performance was about what I expected. Am very glad she did not respond with the equivalent of 52 Pickup.

Am SUPER relieved that my cats and golem are the same ones I left behind. Am going downstairs to check in with Mom.

Later

Interesting developments! I think this is more or less the world I left, but . . . well, not exactly.

I'd found Mom (who looks the same, thank cheeses) and gotten a few pertinent questions answered. It went a little something like this:

ME: Hey, Patti, what's my name?

MOM: [Recognizing and falling in with routine.] Emily!

ME: What do you brush your teeth with?

M: Toothpaste!

ME: Complete this sentence: Centipedes are often found . . .

M: . . . in my daughter's bedroom lab!

ME: So far, so good. . . . [Choking abruptly.] Hey . . . didn't you use to have an aquarium over there near the TV?

M: [Looking at me funny.] A <u>terrarium</u>, sure. Still have one. Remember, an <u>aquarium</u> is for water, and . . .

ME: [Slightly strangled.] I know the difference, Patti . . . it's just . . . ha ha, silly me . . . I guess I forgot that your pet fish were the flying variety.

It is indeed a slightly different world than the one I left, but I'm gonna stay here, maybe look up some of Sweetie-Pie's descendants and see what they're up to these days. Good Stuff, I'm betting.

Mom with a few of Meryl's descendants.

Later

Have checked in with Wilson at his All-Purpose Emporium of Stuff.[63] Truly champion curmudgeon, that Wilson.[64] Unfortunately, all my travels have taken up no time at all here in the present, and I am still six to eight weeks away from my special orders arriving. As Wilson sarcastically pointed out.

Later

Have confronted Great-Aunt Millie about all this Dark Girl stuff. Here's how that went:

ME: Yo, Aunt Millie! What's with all this Dark Girl stuff? I mean, am I really one?

GREAT-AUNT MILLIE: [Looking sheepish.] Yourrr motherrrr and I thinnnk ssssoooo, yessssss.

ME: Well, flibfarx! Couldn't you guys have just told me so in the first place?

GAM: [Long pause.] . . . Noooooo.

ME: Oh, my cheeks. I suppose you and Mom engineered all that mystery around Great-Aunt Lily's death, and

---

63 Not its actual name. Too bad!!!

64 And therefore One of the Good Ones, in my book.

the Dark Aunts, and the Heirloom, and EVERY-
THING, just to get me interested in the family
history?

GAM: [Long pause.] . . . Yessssss.

ME: [Sighing.] K, I guess I'm not the world's easiest
student, but seriously, next time, let's try a little
straight-up HONESTY, what do you say?

GAM: We'lllll seeeee howww it goessss.

ME: [Remembering Respect for Aunties.] All right,
well, I'll try to deserve some honesty, how's that?

GAM: Betterrrrrrrr.

ME: So on that note . . . am I ever gonna get my own
black rock?

GAM: In alllllll honessssty, Emmmilllyyyyy, that is up
to youuuuuuuuuuuu and youuuuu aloooone!

ME: [Shoulda known I'd get a non-answer like that.]
Kayyyy . . . then AT LEAST give me a clue about
those letters we found in the tunnels under Lily's
house. Just one clue, it's all I ask!!!!

GAM: Cerrrrrtainly, myyyyy dearrrrr. My lassssst
name . . . it'ssssss Esssssstrany.

ME: [Light breaking.] M.K., C.U., A.M., M.E.: Mildred
Különös, Camilla Underlig, Amelia Merwürdig,
Millie Estrany! . . . Thanks, Aunt Millie.

> ### NOTE TO SELF:
> Future assignment: Must return to Seasidetown and carve my initials into a chair in the tunnels under Great-Aunt Lily's house!

Later

Have just gotten off the phone with Jakey. Conversation was as follows:

ME: 'Sup, Cousin. Just got back from hanging out with our ancestors.

JAKEY: [Long pause.] [Seriously long pause.] . . . Whoa . . .

ME: AHhahhahhaAHHhah. You get all that?

J: Yeah . . . wow. Great-Grandpa Caleb . . . and Great-Grandma Opal . . . and Uncle Boris . . .

ME: I know, huh?

J: Did I ever tell you that my mom named my parrot Lily cuz it was an old family name?

ME: Whoahhh. . . . Hey, so, you know the worst part of all this, right?

J: Um, wow, I hope you mean the part about you and me being related to Attikol, cuz I can't think of anything worse than that.

ME: On the nose, kid. Look, all of that claptrap aside, could you do me a favor and take a peek inside Attikol's mind, and see if he knows of any living

222

descendants of Lily's family?

J: [Short pause.] [Clearly Attikol is a man of not so much mind.] Hey, that's weird. Yesterday he was hot on your trail . . . and today he believes that Lily's family all died in 1790. What gives?

ME: That, my friend, is what success looks like, thank you very much. One last question: Any future plans in his mind regarding Seasidetown?

J: Well, suddenly he's thinking of taking a trip out there to check some basement for a black potion. Weird!

ME: I expected as much. Well, he won't find anything there, so I guess THAT'S all right.

J: Gotcha. K, well, I guess you owe me one now, right? For telling you about that diary? Huh?

ME: Maybe. Then again, maybe not. I mean, I did talk Great-Grandpa Caleb into taking a hit for you.

J: [Another short pause.] Oh. Wow. Thanks.

ME: Say goodbye to constant surveillance, kiddo!

J: Seriously, though, I keep hoping you'll figure out a way to spring me from this stupid medicine show. Hey, come on, I AM your cousin.

ME: [Sighing.] Don't you think I WANT to help you out?

J: Um, I CAN read your thoughts, remember? I KNOW you think it's handy having a psychic kid hanging out with Attikol, keeping tabs on him for you. But it's not all about you, man! I mean, I haven't seen my mom since I was a year old!

ME: [Mortified.] All right, Cuz, I'm sorry. Look, keep me posted on where you guys go next, and I'm sure I can come up with something, K?

J: K . . . thanks, dude.

Later

Whylime

Glammering jibwax! Just had THEEE most unusual experience in the mudroom. I have met one of my great-nieces!!! I'd taken the Time-Out Machine outdoors for a quick hosing-off and general sterilizing[65] and was just coming back inside when this girl straight up MATERIALIZED in the doorway and totally made me drop my bleach bottle.

ME: AIIIIIEEEEEEEEEE!!!!!

GIRL: Shh, shh, seriously, everything's HJ. I'm a relative of yours. I'm

---

65 Can't risk an anachronistic smallpox outbreak, y'know.

here to help you.

ME: Oh cowcakes. Don't tell me.

G: I came from the future. My name's Whylime. I'm here to keep you from getting stuck forever in the 1790s.

ME: Dude, you're kind of late. I've already been and come back.

WHYLIME: [Snorting.] Did you just say "dude"?

ME: [Snorting right back at her.] Did you say everything was "HJ"?

W: Huckbats! I KNEW I should have brushed up on twenty-first century colloquialisms.

ME: And did you say your name was "Whylime"?

W: Yeah, Whylime. What, you've never heard it? It's been the number one baby name for the past 13 years.

ME: Oh man. That sucks rocks. [Seeing her blank expression.] I mean . . . how regrettable.

W: [Shrugging.] It's HJ now that StarrKeisha is number one.

ME: . . . Whoa.

W: Yeah, all it took was for us to elect StarrKeisha Vasquez-Tantiwittayapitak our very first Thai-Latina double amputee President.

ME: . . . . Whoa. [Slight bleeding from brain.]

W:	Well, sorry I couldn't help you out, Great-Aunt Emily . . . Ummm, actually? I'm supposed to be working on this history report. Do you mind . . . ?
ME:	Not a bit. I've got an incredible collection of twentieth-century punk rock 45s that you may find interesting.
W:	[Suppressing yawn.] HJ . . . or you could just teach me some of your old-timey slang. You know, like "sprocket" and "radtarded."

It's kind of comforting to know that centuries in the future, youth will continue to sneer at their elders' version of coolness. Even so, I had to teach Whylime a lesson on Respect for Aunties. She will be picking spiderwebs out of her teeth and hair for the next week!!!!! Ahhahhahhaaaahhha! Then I gave her some seeds from Lily's garden to use in her Time-Out Machine, and sent her on her way. Her mother is going to LOVE the report she writes on THAT little journey!

Later

Mom has just been in to tell me that I may be able to go back to the 1790s and change the world, but I still have to finish my homework if I want credit for the current school year. Placketjax!

Tomorrow's assignment: Look into getting my GED!!!!

Emily Strange   12/13
Vocabulary List—Extra Credit

1. dracontology—study of lake animals unknown to science
My fondness for Nessie prompted me to major in
dracontology.

2. floccinaucinihilipilification—the act of judging something to
be worthless
Some people consider floccinaucinihilipilification a worthless
use of time, but I disagree wholeheartedly.

3. subfusc—dark and gloomy
It was a subfusc and tempestuous night; suddenly, a shot
rang out . . .

4. anarchipluvian—not rainbow colored
I'll start liking rainbows when they start making them
anarchipluvian.

5. dactylonomy—the art of counting on the fingers
My Oddisee was broken, so I relied on dactylonomy to
complete my calculations.

6. arachibutyrophobia—fear of peanut butter sticking to the roof of the mouth

An intense attack of arachibutyrophobia encouraged me to order egg salad.

7. zenzizenzizenzic—the square of squares squared, or the eighth power of a number

"Zenzizenzizenzic" is number 7 on my vocab list.

8. chthonic—relating to the underworld

Some folks consider Raven to be chthonic just because she was cobbled together out of miscellaneous undead bird parts.

9. transmogrify—to change shape

When I brought the beautiful, innocent butterfly into my home, I had no idea it would soon transmogrify into a snarling, fanged monstrosity and devour us all.

10. daedal—ingenious and complex, intricate, artistically made

Though reasonably daedal, my Time-Out Machine will not be perfect until it is pocket-sized.

11. leucipottomy—the craft of carving white horses onto hillsides

In hindsight, I'm glad my mom decided to teach History of the Strange Family rather than Leucipottomy 101.

12. nixtamalization—process of making hominy from corn

I thank nixtamalization for feeding me on my trip to the 1790s.

13. triskaidekaphilia—fondness for the number 13

Triskaidekaphilia allowed me to enjoy the 13th floor of the hotel all to myself.

Progress Report for Emily Strange
with Self-Evaluations

Current Developments in Particle Physics

Fantastic effort! Have read everything Duntzton library has on the topic. Will need to visit other towns for more literature. Preferably towns that actually have universities.

Advanced Practicum in Krav Maga

As expected, my trainers at Fight Club are very impressed with my skills, and have been clamoring for permission to spar with Raven themselves.[66]

Complex Number Theory

Am turning in top-quality work, but am on thin ice with Professor Mayer after a misguided (but irresistible) booby-trapping of her favorite easy chair. Will probably need to make peace using some of Mom's home-baked cookies!

---

66 However, crushes on Raven are suspected. Permission denied!

Great Poetry of the 13th Century

Will need to take an incomplete this semester. Enjoyed the high adventure of the Nibelungenlied, but got bogged down in the spirituality of Rumi. Will try again when I am feeling more open-minded toward enlightenment.

Fingerpainting

Brilliant work on all assignments. Promoted self to Toepainting next semester.

Music Theory

Have mastered standard tunings for the guitar to Mom's satisfaction. No promises that I will ever actually use them, though.

History of the Strange Family

Participation excellent! Completed all quests and most assignments; turned in 13 points' worth of extra credit. Still much to learn, but good progress all around. Am looking forward to further lessons!!!!

APPENDIX C

Emily Strange
Sept. 6
History of Strange Family
Expository Essay

My Journey to Blackrock: An Exercise in Futility

Today I went tried to go to Blackrock. Unfortunately, there was nothing there. Great-Aunt Millie says Blackrock has come unmoored in space-time. This made for very little to see and do in Blackrock.

The End

Watch out for Emily's
strangest adventure yet:

Emily®
the Strange
Piece of Mind

13 thought-provoking features of Emily's next diary:

1. The Thought Thief
2. Ancestral enemies (and a few ancestral friends)
3. Modern-day Seasidetown
4. FelinoMobileTranscriptoSpy devices
5. Abandoned souvenir kiosk
6. Jakey's memories
7. Super secret book vault
8. Stolen blueprints
9. Regret Maneuvers A through Z
10. Final exams in Particle Physics and
    How-to with Glue
11. Hero-worshipping engineers
12. The 13th Dark Girl
13. Black rock